NOT TO BE TAKEN AT BED-TIME

Not to Be Taken at Bed-Time

& Other Strange Stories

by

Rosa Mulholland

Swan River Press
Dublin, Ireland
MMXXI

Not to Be Taken at Bed-Time
by Rosa Mulholland

Published by
Swan River Press
Dublin, Ireland
in October MMXXI

www.swanriverpress.ie
brian@swanriverpress.ie

Cover design by Meggan Kehrli
from artwork by Brian Coldrick

Set in Garamond by Ken Mackenzie

Published with support from Dublin UNESCO
City of Literature and Dublin City Libraries

ISBN 978-1-78380-752-9

Swan River Press published
a limited hardback edition of
Not to Be Taken at Bed-Time
in April 2019.

Contents

Introduction

In the late-nineteenth century Rosa Mulholland achieved great popularity and acclaim for her many novels (written for both an adult audience and younger readers), several of which chronicled the lives of the Irish poor. These novels, notably *The Wicked Woods of Tobereevil* (1872), incorporated weird elements of Irish folklore. Earlier in her career, she became one of the select band of authors employed by Charles Dickens to write stories for his popular magazine *All the Year Round*, together with Wilkie Collins, Elizabeth Gaskell, Joseph Sheridan Le Fanu, Hesba Stretton, and Amelia B. Edwards.

She was born in Belfast on 19 March 1841, the second daughter of a doctor (Joseph Stevenson Mulholland) whose family had become prosperous from textile manufacture. She was educated at home and studied art in South Kensington.

While living in London, Rosa published her first novel, *Dunmara* (1864), under the pseudonym "Ruth Murray", and was personally encouraged by Dickens to begin contributing regularly to his bestselling weekly *All the Year Round*.

She wrote "Another Past Lodger Relates His Experience as a Poor Relation", the third chapter of *Mrs. Lirriper's Legacy*, the 1864 Christmas Number (which also contained Amelia B. Edwards' classic "The Phantom Coach"), followed by "Not to be Taken at Bed-Time" for the 1865 Christmas Number, *Doctor Marigold's Prescriptions*. This memorable Irish witchcraft horror tale became her best-known story following its appearance in *The Supernatural Omnibus*, edited by Montague Summers in 1931 and much reprinted.

"Not to be Taken at Bed-Time" was closely followed by two of Rosa Mulholland's best ghost stories, "The Ghost at the Rath" (14 April 1866) and "The Haunted Organist of Hurly Burly" (19 November 1866).

Dickens serialised her novella "The Late Miss Hollingford" in *All the Year Round* from 4 April to 2 May 1868, and it was immediately reprinted in a Tauchnitz edition together with *No Thoroughfare* by Charles Dickens and Wilkie Collins. As "The Late Miss Hollingford" was not credited to any specific author, it was wrongly assumed by many readers to be the work of Dickens and Collins until it was eventually published separately in book form under Rosa Mulholland's name in 1886.

Her next novel, *Hester's History*, was serialised in *All the Year Round* from 29 August to 28 November 1868, and published in book form (as by R.M.) in 1869.

After Dickens died in 1870, Rosa Mulholland continued to write many stories for *All the Year Round*, notably "The Signor John" (Christmas 1871), "A Will o' the Wisp" (Christmas 1872), and "The Country Cousin" (16 and 23 May 1874).

During the 1870s she began a productive career as a children's writer, and these books are her most collectable and sought after today: *The Little Flower Seekers, being adventures of Troy and Daisy in a Wonderful Garden by Moonlight* (1871), richly illustrated by W. H. Frith, W. French, and F. E. Hulme; *The First Christmas for Our Dear Little Ones* (1875), with fifteen colour wood-engravings painted by L. Diefenback "richly executed in xylography", and verse texts by Rosa Mulholland telling the Nativity story beneath each picture; and *Puck and Blossom* (1875), one of the earliest books to be illustrated by Kate Greenaway.

Among Rosa Mulholland's later stories for *All the Year Round* were three notable examples written for the special "Extra Summer Numbers"; "The Mystery of Ora" (1 July 1879), a memorable supernatural tale, not reprinted until 2013; "A Strange Love Story" (3 July 1882), featuring reincarnation; and "The Hungry Death" (1 July 1880), a graphic macabre tale set on a remote Irish island during the 1840s famine.

When Rosa Mulholland left London to settle permanently in Dublin in the 1870s, she befriended Father Matthew Russell, S. J., who edited the *Irish Monthly*, and whose brother Francis (later Lord Russell of Killowen) was married to her elder sister Ellen Clare Mulholland, author of a dozen children's books from *The Little Bogtrotten* (1878) to *Terence O'Neill's Heiress* (1909).

Most of Rosa Mulholland's later novels and short stories were set in rural Ireland, and many achieved a wide readership in the pages of *Irish Monthly* from "The Strange Schooner" (June 1876) to "A Scrap of Irish Folklore" (December 1894), in which a man returns from the grave (with the ghosts of two children) and kisses his widow, leaving her lips permanently blue and ice-cold.

"The Girl Under the Lake" (August-December 1881), a fantasy describing the adventures of a fairy who escapes from an underwater domain in Lough Neagh and loses her wings, was reprinted in her very scarce collection, *The Walking Trees, and other tales* (M. H. Gill, 1885 [1884]), and several of her *All the Year Round* stories were collected in *The Haunted Organist of Hurly Burly* (Hutchinson [1891]).

Rosa Mulholland continued to write seasonal strange stories for the Christmas Numbers of London magazines, including "The Old Stain on the Floor" (*Yule Tide*, 1884); "The Ghost of Wildwood Chase", another tale of reincarnation (*Illustrated Almanac & Annual*, 1888); and a final ghost story, "The Lady Tantivy" (*Temple Bar*, January 1898).

Two of her most popular and widely acclaimed adult Irish novels were both published by Kegan Paul in 1886: *Marcella Grace* (originally serialised in *Irish Monthly* in 1885), and *A Fair Emigrant*, dealing with the heroine's emigration from Ireland to America.

In 1891 Rosa Mulholland married the eminent Irish historian John T. Gilbert (1829-1898), whose imposing house Villa Nova at Blackrock (near Dublin) was filled with his unique collection of Irish historical and archaeological works. Among his many important books were the *History of the City of Dublin* (1861) and the seven-volume *History of the Irish Confederation* (1882-91). He died in May 1898, a year after receiving his knighthood. His widow wrote a two-volume biography, *The Life of Sir John T. Gilbert: Irish Historian and Archivist* (1905). She donated his magnificent collection of books and manuscripts, containing many valuable and important historical items, to the City of Dublin corporation.

Rosa Mulholland remained very busy producing a long line of novels mostly set in rural Ireland and featuring strong, independent female characters. Over a dozen of these were published by Blackie in similar format to their G. A. Henty volumes bound in handsome decorated cloth with olivine edges, and frequently given away as school prizes.

Among these very popular Blackie novels were *Banshee Castle* (1895), describing the adventures of three girls who move from Kensington to their old family estate in the West of Ireland, where they hear many curious tales from the local folklore; *Cynthia's Bonnet Shop* (1901), in which two poor Irish sisters open a milliner's shop in London to support their invalid mother; *A Girl's Ideal* (1905), with an American heiress trying to spend her fortune to help good causes in Ireland; *Cousin Sara* (1909); *The O'Shaughnessy Girls* (1911); *Twin Sisters* (1911); *Fair Noreen* (1912); *The Daughter in Possession* (1915); and *Narcissa's Ring* (1916).

She also wrote three collections of poetry, *Vagrant Verses* (1886 & 1899), *Spirit and Dust* (1908), and *Dreams and Realities* (1916).

Rosa Mulholland, Lady Gilbert, died in her 80th year at Villa Nova on 21 April 1921.

By the late 1920s all of her once bestselling novels had gone out-of-print, and sadly she was soon forgotten. Unlike her husband, she failed to gain entry into the original and modern editions of *Dictionary of National Biography*.

Her best seven supernatural and weird short stories have never been gathered together in one volume before, and the present collection seeks to remedy the gap to celebrate this gifted late Victorian "Mistress of the Macabre".

Richard Dalby
Scarborough
North Yorkshire

Not to Be Taken at Bed-Time

Not to Be Taken at Bed-Time

This is the legend of a house called the Devil's Inn, standing in the heather on the top of the Connemara mountains, in a shallow valley hollowed between five peaks. Tourists sometimes come in sight of it on September evenings; a crazy and weather-stained apparition, with the sun glaring at it angrily between the hills, and striking its shattered window-panes. Guides are known to shun it, however.

The house was built by a stranger, who came no one knew whence, and whom the people nicknamed Coll Dhu (Black Coll), because of his sullen bearing and solitary habits. His dwelling they called the Devil's Inn, because no tired traveller had ever been asked to rest under its roof, nor friend known to cross its threshold. No one bore him company in his retreat but a wizen-faced old man, who shunned the good-morrow of the trudging peasant when he made occasional excursions to the nearest village for provisions for himself and master, and who was as secret as a stone concerning all the antecedents of both.

For the first year of their residence in the country, there had been much speculation as to who they were, and what they did with themselves up there among the clouds and eagles. Some said that Coll Dhu was a scion of the old family from whose hands the surrounding lands had passed; and that, embittered by poverty and pride, he had come to bury himself in solitude, and brood over his misfortunes.

Others hinted of crime, and flight from another country; others again whispered of those who were cursed from their birth, and could never smile, nor yet make friends with a fellow-creature till the day of their death. But when two years had passed, the wonder had somewhat died out, and Coll Dhu was little thought of, except when a shepherd looking for sheep crossed the track of a big dark man walking the mountains gun in hand, to whom he did not dare say "Lord save you!" or when a housewife rocking the cradle of a winter's night, crossed herself as a gust of a storm thundered over her cabin-roof, with the exclamation, "Oh, then, it's Coll Dhu that has enough o' the fresh air about his head up there this night, the creature!"

Coll Dhu had lived thus in his solitude for some years, when it became known that Colonel Blake, the new lord of the soil, was coming to visit the country. By climbing one of the peaks encircling his eyrie, Coll could look sheer down a mountain-side, and see in miniature beneath him, a grey old dwelling with ivied chimneys and weather-slated walls, standing amongst straggling trees and grim warlike rocks, that gave it the look of a fortress, gazing out to the Atlantic for ever with the eager eyes of all its windows, as if demanding perpetually, "What tidings from the New World?"

He could see now masons and carpenters crawling about below, like ants in the sun, over-running the old house from base to chimney, daubing here and knocking there, tumbling down walls that looked to Coll, up among the clouds, like a handful of jack-stones, and building up others that looked like the toy fences in a child's farm. Throughout several months he must have watched the busy ants at their task of breaking and mending again, disfiguring and beautifying; but when all was done he had not the curiosity to stride down and admire the handsome panelling of the new billiard-room, nor yet the fine view which the enlarged bay-window in the drawing-room commanded of the watery highway to Newfoundland.

Deep summer was melting into autumn, and the amber streaks of decay were beginning to creep out and trail over the ripe purple of moor and mountain, when Colonel Blake, his only daughter, and a party of friends, arrived in the country. The grey house below was alive with gaiety, but Coll Dhu no longer found an interest in observing from his eyrie. When he watched the sun rise or set, he chose to ascend some crag that looked on no human habitation. When he sallied forth on his excursions, gun in hand, he set his face towards the most isolated wastes, dipping into the loneliest valleys, and scaling the nakedest ridges. When he came by chance within call of other excursionists, gun in hand he plunged into the shade of some hollow, and avoided an encounter. Yet it was fated, for all that, that he and Colonel Blake should meet.

Towards the evening of one bright September day, the wind changed, and in half an hour the mountains were wrapped in a thick blinding mist. Coll Dhu was far from his den, but so well had he searched these mountains, and inured himself to their climate, that neither storm, rain, nor fog, had power to disturb him. But while he stalked on his way, a faint and agonised cry from a human voice reached him through the smothering mist. He quickly tracked the sound, and gained the side of a man who was stumbling along in danger of death at every step.

"Follow me!" said Coll Dhu to this man, and, in an hour's time, brought him safely to the lowlands, and up to the walls of the eager-eyed mansion.

"I am Colonel Blake," said the frank soldier, when, having left the fog behind them, they stood in the starlight under the lighted windows. "Pray tell me quickly to whom I owe my life."

As he spoke, he glanced up at his benefactor, a large man with a sombre sun-burned face.

"Colonel Blake," said Coll Dhu, after a strange pause, "your father suggested to my father to stake his estates at the gaming-table. They were staked, and the tempter won. Both are dead; but you and I live, and I have sworn to injure you."

The colonel laughed good humouredly at the uneasy face above him.

"And you began to keep your oath tonight by saving my life?" said he. "Come! I am a soldier, and know how to meet an enemy; but I had far rather meet a friend. I shall not be happy till you have eaten my salt. We have merrymaking tonight in honour of my daughter's birthday. Come in and join us?"

Coll Dhu looked at the earth doggedly.

"I have told you," he said, "who and what I am, and I will not cross your threshold."

But at this moment (so runs the story) a French window opened among the flower-beds by which they were standing, and a vision appeared which stayed the words on Coll's tongue. A stately girl, clad in white satin, stood framed in the ivied window, with the warm light from within streaming around her richly-moulded figure into the night. Her face was as pale as her gown, her eyes were swimming in tears, but a firm smile sat on her lips as she held out both hands to her father. The light behind her touched the glistening folds of her dress—the lustrous pearls round her throat—the coronet of blood-red roses which encircled the knotted braids at the back of her head. Satin, pearls, and roses—had Coll Dhu, of the Devil's Inn, never set eyes upon such things before?

Evleen Blake was no nervous tearful miss. A few quick words—"Thank God! you're safe; the rest have been home an hour"—and a tight pressure of her father's fingers between her own jewelled hands, were all that betrayed the uneasiness she had suffered.

"Faith, my love, I owe my life to this brave gentleman!" said the blithe colonel. "Press him to come in and be our guest, Evleen. He wants to retreat to his mountains, and lose himself again in the fog where I found him; or, rather, where he found me! Come, sir" (to Coll), "you must surrender to this fair besieger."

An introduction followed. "Coll Dhu!" murmured Evleen Blake, for she had heard the common tales of him; but with a frank welcome she invited her father's preserver to taste the hospitality of that father's house.

"I beg you to come in, sir," she said; "but for you our gaiety must have been turned into mourning. A shadow will be upon our mirth if our benefactor disdains to join in it."

With a sweet grace, mingled with a certain hauteur from which she was never free, she extended her white hand to the tall looming figure outside the window; to have it grasped and wrung in a way that made the proud girl's eyes flash their amazement, and the same little hand clench itself in displeasure, when it had hid itself like an outraged thing among the shining folds of her gown. Was this Coll Dhu mad, or rude?

The guest no longer refused to enter, but followed the white figure into a little study where a lamp burned; and the gloomy stranger, the bluff colonel, and the young mistress of the house, were fully discovered to each other's eyes. Evleen glanced at the newcomer's dark face, and shuddered with a feeling of indescribable dread and dislike; then, to her father, accounted for the shudder after a popular fashion, saying lightly: "There is someone walking over my grave."

So Coll Dhu was present at Evleen Blake's birthday ball. Here he was, under a roof which ought to have been his own, a stranger, known only by a nickname, shunned and solitary. Here he was, who had lived among the eagles and foxes, lying in wait with a fell purpose, to be revenged on the son of his father's foe for poverty and disgrace, for the broken heart of a dead mother, for the loss of a self-slaughtered father, for the dreary scattering of brothers and sisters. Here he stood, a Samson shorn of his strength; and all because a haughty girl had melting eyes, a winning mouth, and looked radiant in satin and roses.

Peerless where many were lovely, she moved among her friends, trying to be unconscious of the gloomy fire of those strange eyes which followed her unweariedly wherever she went. And when her father begged her to be gracious to the unsocial guest whom he would fain conciliate, she courteously conducted him to the new picture-gallery adjoining the drawing-rooms; explained under what odd circumstances the colonel had picked up this little painting or that; using every delicate art her pride would allow to achieve her father's purpose, whilst maintaining at the same time her own personal reserve; trying to divert the guest's oppressive attention from herself to the objects for which she claimed his notice. Coll Dhu followed his conductress and listened to her voice, but what she said mattered nothing; nor did she wring many words of comment or reply from his lips, until they paused in a retired corner where the light was dim, before a window from which the curtain was withdrawn. The sashes were open, and nothing was visible but water; the night Atlantic, with the full moon riding high above a bank of clouds, making silvery tracks outward towards the distance of infinite mystery dividing two worlds. Here the following little scene is said to have been enacted.

"This window of my father's own planning, is it not creditable to his taste?" said the young hostess, as she stood, herself glittering like a dream of beauty, looking on the moonlight.

Coll Dhu made no answer; but suddenly, it is said, asked her for a rose from a cluster of flowers that nestled in the lace on her bosom.

For the second time that night Evleen Blake's eyes flashed with no gentle light. But this man was the saviour of her father. She broke off a blossom, and with such good grace, and also with such queen-like dignity as she might assume, presented it to him. Whereupon, not only was the rose seized, but also the hand that gave it, which was hastily covered with kisses.

Then her anger burst upon him.

"Sir," she cried, "if you are a gentleman you must be mad! If you are not mad, then you are not a gentleman!"

"Be merciful," said Coll Dhu; "I love you. My God, I never loved a woman before! Ah!" he cried, as a look of disgust crept over her face, "you hate me. You shuddered the first time your eyes met mine. I love you, and you hate me!"

"I do," cried Evleen, vehemently, forgetting everything but her indignation. "Your presence is like something evil to me. Love me?—your looks poison me. Pray, sir, talk no more to me in this strain."

"I will trouble you no longer," said Coll Dhu. And, stalking to the window, he placed one powerful hand upon the sash, and vaulted from it out of her sight.

Bare-headed as he was, Coll Dhu strode off to the mountains, but not towards his own home. All the remaining dark hours of that night he is believed to have walked the labyrinths of the hills, until dawn began to scatter the clouds with a high wind. Fasting, and on foot from sunrise the morning before, he was then glad enough to see a cabin right in his way. Walking in, he asked for water to drink, and a corner where he might throw himself to rest.

There was a wake in the house, and the kitchen was full of people, all wearied out with the night's watch; old men were dozing over their pipes in the chimney-corner, and here and there a woman was fast asleep with her head on a neighbour's knee. All who were awake crossed themselves when Coll Dhu's figure darkened the door, because of his evil name; but an old man of the house invited him in, and offering him milk, and promising him a roasted potato by-and-by, conducted him to a small room off the kitchen, one end of which was strewed with heather, and where there were only two women sitting gossiping over a fire.

"A thraveller," said the old man, nodding his head at the women, who nodded back, as if to say "he has the traveller's right." And Coll Dhu flung himself on the heather, in the furthest corner of the narrow room.

The women suspended their talk for a while; but presently, guessing the intruder to be asleep, resumed it in voices above a whisper. There was but a patch of window with the grey dawn behind it, but Coll could see the figures by the firelight over which they bent: an old woman sitting forward with her withered hands extended to the embers, and a girl reclining against the hearth wall, with her healthy face, bright eyes, and crimson draperies, glowing by turns in the flickering blaze.

"I do' know," said the girl, "but it's the quarest marriage iver I h'ard of. Sure, it's not three weeks since he tould right an' left that he hated her like poison!"

"Whist, asthoreen!" said the colliagh, bending forward confidentially; "throth an' we all know that o' him. But what could he do, the crature! When she put the burragh-bos on him!"

"The *what*?" asked the girl.

"Then the burragh-bos machree-o? That's the spanchel o' death, avourneen; an' well she has him tethered to her now, bad luck to her!"

The old woman rocked herself and stifled the Irish cry breaking from her wrinkled lips by burying her face in her cloak.

"But what is it?" asked the girl, eagerly. "What's the burragh-bos, anyways, an' where did she get it?"

"Och, och! it's not fit for comin' over to young ears, but cuggir (whisper), acushla! It's a sthrip o' the skin o' a corpse, peeled from the crown o' the head to the heel, without crack or split, or the charm's broke; an' that, rowled up, and put on a sthring roun' the neck o' the wan that's cowld by the wan that wants to be loved. An' sure enough it puts the fire in their hearts, hot an' sthrong, afore twinty-four hours is gone."

The girl had started from her lazy attitude, and gazed at her companion with eyes dilated by horror.

"Marciful Saviour!" she cried. "Not a sowl on airth would bring the curse out o' heaven by sich a black doin'!"

"Aisy, Biddeen alanna! an' there's wan that does it, an' isn't the devil. Arrah, asthoreen, did ye niver hear tell o' Pexie na Pishrogie, that lives betune two hills o' Maam Turk?"

"I h'ard o' her," said the girl, breathlessly.

"Well, sorra bit lie, but it's hersel' that does it. She'll do it for money any day. Sure they hunted her from the graveyard o' Salruck, where she had the dead raised; an' glory be to God! they would ha' murthered her, only they missed her thracks, an' couldn't bring it home to her afther."

"Whist, a-wauher" (my mother)," said the girl; "here's the thraveller getting up to set off on his road again! Och, then, it's the short rest he tuk, the sowl!"

It was enough for Coll, however. He had got up, and now went back to the kitchen, where the old man had caused a dish of potatoes to be roasted, and earnestly pressed his visitor to sit down and eat of them. This Coll did readily; having recruited his strength by a meal, he betook himself to the mountains again, just as the rising sun was flashing among the waterfalls, and sending the night mists drifting down the glens. By sundown the same evening he was striding over the hills of Maam Turk, asking of shepherds his way to the cabin of one Pexie na Pishrogie.

In a hovel on a brown desolate heath, with scared-looking hills flying off into the distance on every side, he found Pexie: a yellow-faced hag, dressed in a dark-red blanket, with elf-locks of coarse black hair protruding from under an orange kerchief swathed round her wrinkled jaws. She was bending over a pot upon her fire, where herbs were simmering, and she looked up with an evil glance when Coll Dhu darkened her door.

"The burragh-bos is it her honour wants?" she asked, when he had made known his errand.

"Ay, ay; but the arrighad, the arrighad (money) for Pexie. The burragh-bos is ill to get."

"I will pay," said Coll Dhu, laying a sovereign on the bench before her.

The witch sprang upon it, and chuckling, bestowed on her visitor a glance which made even Coll Dhu shudder.

"Her honour is a fine king," she said, "an' her is fit to get the burragh-bos. Ha! Ha! her sall get the burragh-bos from Pexie. But the arrighad is not enough. More, more!"

She stretched out her claw-like hand, and Coll dropped another sovereign into it. Whereupon she fell into more horrible convulsions of delight.

"Hark ye!" cried Coll. "I have paid you well, but if your infernal charm does not work, I will have you hunted for a witch!"

"Work!" cried Pexie, rolling up her eyes. "If Pexie's charm not work, then her honour come back here an' carry these bits o' mountain away on her back. Ay, her will work. If the colleen hate her honour like the old diaoul hersel', still an' withal her love will love her honour like her own white sowl afore the sun sets or rises. That (with a furtive leer), or the colleen dhas go wild mad afore wan hour."

"Hag!" returned Coll Dhu; "the last part is a hellish invention of your own. I heard nothing of madness. If you want more money, speak out, but play none of your hideous tricks on me."

The witch fixed her cunning eyes on him, and took her cue at once from his passion.

"Her honour guess thrue," she simpered; "it is only the little bit more arrighad poor Pexie want."

Again the skinny hand was extended. Coll Dhu shrank from touching it, and threw his gold coin upon the table.

"King, king!" chuckled Pexie. "Her honour is a grand king. Her honour is fit to get the burragh-bos. The colleen dhas sall love her like her own white sowl. Ha, ha!"

"When shall I get it?" asked Coll Dhu, impatiently.

"Her honour sall come back to Pexie in so many days, do-deag (twelve), so many days, fur that the burragh-bos is hard to get. The lonely graveyard is far away, an' the dead man is hard to raise—"

"Silence!" cried Coll Dhu; "not a word more. I will have your hideous charm, but what it is, or where you get it, I will not know."

Then, promising to come back in twelve days, he took his departure. Turning to look back when a little way across the heath, he saw Pexie gazing after him, standing on her black hill in relief against the lurid flames of the dawn, seeming to his dark imagination like a fury with all hell at her back.

At the appointed time Coll Dhu got the promised charm. He sewed it with perfumes into a cover of cloth of gold, and slung it to a fine-wrought chain. Lying in a casket which had once held the jewels of Coll's broken-hearted mother, it looked a glittering bauble enough. Meantime the people of the mountains were cursing over their cabin fires, because there had been another unholy raid upon their graveyard, and were banding themselves to hunt the criminal down.

A fortnight passed. How or where could Coll Dhu find an opportunity to put the charm round the neck of the colonel's proud daughter? More gold was dropped into Pexie's greedy claw, and then she promised to assist him in his dilemma.

Next morning the witch dressed herself in decent garb, smoothed her elf-locks under a snowy cap, smoothed the wrinkles out of her face, and with a basket on her arm locked the door of the hovel, and took her way to the lowlands. Pexie seemed to have given up her disreputable calling for that of a simple mushroom-gatherer. The housekeeper at the grey house bought poor Muireade's mushrooms off her every morning. Every morning she left unfailingly a nosegay of wild flowers for Miss Evleen Blake, "God bless her! She had never seen the darling young lady with her own two longing eyes, but sure hadn't she heard tell of her sweet purty face, miles away!" And at last, one morning, whom should she meet but Miss Evleen herself returning alone from a ramble. Whereupon poor Muireade "made bold" to present her flowers in person.

"Ah," said Evleen, "it is you who leave me the flowers every morning? They are very sweet."

Muireade had sought her only for a look at her beautiful face. And now that she had seen it, as bright as the sun, and as fair as the lily, she would take up her basket and go away contented.

Yet she lingered a little longer.

"My lady never walk up big mountain?" said Pexie.

"No," said Evleen, laughing; she feared she could not walk up a mountain.

"Ah yes; my lady ought to go, with more gran' ladies an' gentlemen, ridin' on purty little donkeys, up the big mountains. Oh, gran' things up big mountains for my lady to see!"

Thus she set to work, and kept her listener enchained for an hour, while she related wonderful stories of those upper regions. And as Evleen looked up to the burly crowns of the hills, perhaps she thought there might be sense in this wild old woman's suggestion. It ought to be a grand world up yonder.

Be that as it may, it was not long after this when Coll Dhu got notice that a party from the grey house would explore the mountains next day; that Evleen Blake would be one of the number; and that he, Coll, must prepare to house and refresh a crowd of weary people, who in the evening should be brought, hungry and faint, to his door. The simple mushroom-gatherer should be discovered laying in her humble stock among the green places between the hills, should volunteer to act as guide to the party, should lead them far out of their way through the mountains and up and down the most toilsome ascents and across dangerous places; to escape safely from which, the servants should be told to throw away the baskets of provisions which they carried.

Coll Dhu was not idle. Such a feast was set forth, as had never been spread so near the clouds before. We are told of wonderful dishes furnished by unwholesome agency, and from a place believed much hotter than is necessary for purposes of cookery. We are told also how Coll Dhu's barren chambers were suddenly hung with curtains of velvet, and with fringes of gold; how the blank white walls glowed with delicate colours and gilding; how gems of pictures sprang into sight between the panels; how the tables blazed with plate and gold, and glittered with the rarest glass; how such wines flowed, as the guests had never tasted; how servants in the richest livery, amongst whom the wizen-faced old man was a mere nonentity, appeared, and stood ready to carry in the wonderful dishes, at whose extraordinary fragrance the eagles came pecking to the windows, and the foxes drew near the walls, snuffing. Sure enough, in all good time, the weary party came within sight of the Devil's Inn, and Coll Dhu sallied forth to invite them across his lonely threshold. Colonel Blake (to whom Evleen, in her delicacy, had said no word of the solitary's strange behaviour to herself) hailed his appearance with delight, and the whole party sat down to Coll's banquet in high good humour. Also, it is said, in much amazement at the magnificence of the mountain recluse.

All went in to Coll's feast, save Evleen Blake, who remained standing on the threshold of the outer door; weary, but unwilling to rest there; hungry, but unwilling to eat there. Her white cambric dress was gathered on her arms, crushed and sullied with the toils of the day; her bright cheek was a little sun-burned; her small dark head with its braids a little tossed, was bared to the mountain air and the glory of the sinking sun; her hands were loosely tangled in the strings of her hat; and her foot sometimes tapped the threshold-stone. So she was seen.

The peasants tell that Coll Dhu and her father came praying her to enter, and that the magnificent servants brought viands to the threshold; but no step would she move inward, no morsel would she taste.

"Poison, poison!" she murmured, and threw the food in handfuls to the foxes, who were snuffing on the heath.

But it was different when Muireade, the kindly old woman, the simple mushroom-gatherer, with all the wicked wrinkles smoothed out of her face, came to the side of the hungry girl, and coaxingly presented a savoury mess of her own sweet mushrooms, served on a common earthen platter.

"An' darlin', my lady, poor Muireade her cook them hersel', an' no thing o' this house touch them or look at poor Muireade's mushrooms."

Then Evleen took the platter and ate a delicious meal. Scarcely was it finished when a heavy drowsiness fell upon her, and, unable to sustain herself on her feet, she presently sat down upon the door-stone. Leaning her head against the framework of the door, she was soon in a deep sleep, or trance. So she was found.

"Whimsical, obstinate little girl!" said the colonel, putting his hand on the beautiful slumbering head. And taking her in his arms he carried her into a chamber which had been (say the story-tellers) nothing but a bare and sorry closet in the morning but which was now fitted up with Oriental splendour. And here on a luxurious couch she was laid, with a crimson coverlet wrapping her feet. And here in the tempered light coming through jewelled glass, where yesterday had been a coarse rough-hung window, her father looked his last upon her lovely face.

The colonel returned to his host and friends, and by-and-by the whole party sallied forth to see the after-glare of a fierce sunset swathing the hills in flames. It was not until they had gone some distance that Coll Dhu remembered to go back and fetch his telescope. He was not long absent. But he was absent long enough to enter that glowing chamber with a stealthy step, to throw a light chain around the neck of the sleeping girl, and to slip among the folds of her dress the hideous glittering burragh-bos.

After he had gone away again, Pexie came stealing to the door, and, opening it a little, sat down on the mat outside, with her cloak wrapped round her. An hour passed, and Evleen Blake still slept, her breathing scarcely stirring the deadly bauble on her breast. After that, she began to murmur and moan and Pexie pricked up her ears. Presently a sound in the room told her that the victim was awake and had risen. Then Pexie put her face to the aperture of the door and looked in, gave a howl of dismay, and fled from the house, to be seen in that country no more.

The light was fading among the hills, and the ramblers were returning towards the Devil's Inn, when a group of ladies who were considerably in advance of the rest, met Evleen Blake advancing towards them on the heath, with her hair disordered as by sleep, and no covering on her head. They noticed something bright, like gold, shifting and glancing with the motion of her figure. There had been some jesting among them about Evleen's fancy for falling asleep on the door-step instead of coming in to dinner, and they advanced laughing, to rally her on the subject.

But she stared at them in a strange way, as if she did not know them, and passed on. Her friends were rather offended, and commented on her fantastic humour; only one looked after her, and got laughed at by her companions for expressing uneasiness on the wilful young lady's account.

So they kept their way, and the solitary figure went fluttering on, the white robe blushing, and the fatal burragh-bos glittering in the reflection from the sky. A hare crossed her path, and she laughed out loudly, and clapping her hands, sprang after it. Then she stopped and asked questions of the stones, striking them with her open palm because they would not answer. (An amazed shepherd sitting behind a rock witnessed these strange proceedings.) By-and-by she began to call after the birds, in a wild shrill way startling the echoes of the hills as she went along. A party of gentlemen returning by a dangerous path, heard the unusual sound and stopped to listen.

"What is that?" asked one.

"A young eagle," said Coll Dhu, whose face had become livid, "they often give such cries."

"It was uncommonly like a woman's voice!" was the reply; and immediately another wild note rang towards them from the rocks above; a bare saw-like ridge, shelving away to some distance ahead, and projecting one hungry tooth over an abyss. A few more moments and they saw Evleen Blake's light figure fluttering out towards this dizzy point.

"My Evleen!" cried the colonel, recognising his daughter, "she is mad to venture on such a spot!"

"Mad!" repeated Coll Dhu. And then he dashed off to the rescue with all the might and swiftness of his powerful limbs.

When he drew near her, Evleen had almost reached the verge of the terrible rock. Very cautiously he approached her, his object being to seize her in his strong arms before she was aware of his presence, and carry her many yards away from the spot of danger. But in a fatal moment Evleen turned her head and saw him. One wild ringing cry of hate and horror, which startled the very eagles and scattered a flight of curlews above her head, broke from her lips. A step backward brought her within a foot of death.

One desperate though wary stride, and she was struggling in Coll's embrace. One glance in her eyes, and he saw that he was striving with a mad woman. Back, back, she dragged him, and he had nothing to grasp by. The rock was slippery and his shod feet would not cling to it. Back, back! A hoarse panting, a dire swinging to and fro; and then the rock was standing naked against the sky, no one was there, and Coll Dhu and Evleen Blake lay shattered far below.

The Ghost at the Rath

Many may disbelieve this story, yet there are some still living who can remember hearing, when children, of the events which it details, and of the strange sensation which their publicity excited. The tale, in its present form, is copied, by permission, from a memoir written by the chief actor in the romance, and preserved as a sort of heirloom in the family whom it concerns.

In the year —— I, John Thunder, Captain in the —— Regiment, having passed many years abroad following my profession, received notice that I had become owner of certain properties which I had never thought to inherit. I set off for my native land, arrived in Dublin, found that my good fortune was real, and at once began to look about me for old friends. The first I met with, quite by accident, was curly-headed Frank O'Brien, who had been at school with me, though I was ten years his senior. He was curly-headed still, and handsome, as he had promised to be, but careworn and poor. During an evening spent at his chambers I drew all his history from him. He was a briefless barrister. As a man he was not more talented than he had been as a boy. Hard work and anxiety had not brought him success, only broken his health and soured his mind. He was in love, and he could not marry. I soon knew all about Mary Leonard, his *fiancée*, whom he had met at a house in the country somewhere, in which she was governess. They had now been engaged for two years—she active and hopeful, he sick and despondent. From the letters of hers which he showed me, I thought she was worth all the devotion he felt for her. I considered a good deal about what could be done for Frank, but I could not easily hit upon a plan to assist him. For ten chances you have of helping a sharp man, you have not two for a dull one.

In the meantime my friend must regain his health, and a change of air and scenery was necessary. I urged him to make a voyage of discovery to the Rath, an old house and park which had come into my possession as portion of my recently acquired estates. I had never been to the place myself; but it had once been the residence of Sir Luke Thunder, of generous memory, and I knew that it was furnished, and provided with a caretaker. I pressed him to leave Dublin at once, and promised to follow him as soon as I found it possible to do so.

So Frank went down to the Rath. The place was two hundred miles away; he was a stranger there, and far from well. When the first week came to an end, and I had heard nothing from him, I did not like the silence; when a fortnight had passed, and still not a word to say he was alive, I felt decidedly uncomfortable; and when the third week of his absence arrived at Saturday without bringing me news, I found myself whizzing through a part of the country I had never travelled before, in the same train in which I had seen Frank seated at our parting.

I reached D——, and, shouldering my knapsack, walked right into the heart of a lovely wooded country. Following the directions I had received, I made my way to a lonely road, on which I met not a soul, and which seemed cut out of the heart of a forest, so closely were the trees ranked on either side, and so dense was the twilight made by the meeting and intertwining of the thick branches overhead. In these shades I came upon a gate, like a gate run to seed, with tall, thin, brick pillars, brandishing long grasses from their heads, and spotted with a melancholy crust of creeping moss. I jangled a cracked bell, and an old man appeared from the thickets within, stared at me, then admitted me with a rusty key. I breathed freely on hearing that my friend was well and to be seen. I presented a letter to the old man, having a fancy not to avow myself.

I found my friend walking up and down the alleys of a neglected orchard, with the lichened branches tangled above his head, and ripe apples rotting about his feet. His hands were locked behind his back, and his head was set on one side, listening to the singing of a bird. I never had seen him look so well; yet there was a vacancy about his whole air which I did not like. He did not seem at all surprised to see me, asked had he really not written to me; thought he had; was so comfortable that he had forgotten everything else. He fancied he had only been there about three days; could not imagine how the time had passed. He seemed to talk wildly, and this, coupled with the unusual happy placidity of his manner, confounded me. The place knew him, he told me confidentially; the place belonged to him, or should; the birds sang him this, the very trees bent before him as he passed, the air whispered him that he had been long expected, and should be poor no more. Wrestling with my judgement ere it might pronounce him mad, I followed him indoors. The Rath was no ordinary old country-house. The acres around it were so wildly overgrown that it was hard to decide which had been pleasure-ground and where the thickets had begun. The plan of the house was fine, with mullioned windows, and here and there a fleck of stained glass flinging back the challenge of an angry sunset. The vast rooms were full of a dusky glare from the sky as I strolled through them in the twilight. The antique furniture had many a blood-red stain on the abrupt notches of its dark carvings; the dusty mirrors flared back at the windows, while the faded curtains produced streaks of uncertain colour from the depths of their sullen foldings.

Dinner was laid for us in the library, a long wainscoted room, with an enormous fire roaring up the chimney, sending a dancing light over the dingy titles of long unopened books. The old man who had unlocked the gate for me served us at table, and, after drawing the dusty curtains, and furnishing us with a plentiful supply of fuel and wine, left us. His clanking hobnailed shoes went echoing away in the distance over the unmatted tiles of the vacant hall till a door closed with a resounding clang very far away, letting us know that we were shut up together for the night in this vast, mouldy, oppressive old house.

I felt as if I could scarcely breathe in it. I could not eat with my usual appetite. The air of the place seemed heavy and tainted. I grew sick and restless. The very wine tasted badly, as if it had been drugged. I had a strange feeling that I had been in the house before, and that something evil had happened to me in it. Yet such could not be the case. What puzzled me most was, that I should feel dissatisfied at seeing Frank looking so well, and eating so heartily. A little time before I should have been glad to suffer something to see him as he looked now; and yet not quite as he looked now. There was a drowsy contentment about him which I could not understand. He did not talk of his work, or of any wish to return to it. He seemed to have no thought of anything but the delight of hanging about that old house, which had certainly cast a spell over him.

About midnight he seized a light, and proposed retiring to our rooms. "I have such delightful dreams in this place," he said. He volunteered, as we issued into the hall, to take me upstairs and show me the upper regions of his paradise.

I said, "Not to-night." I felt a strange creeping sensation as I looked up the vast black staircase, wide enough for a coach to drive down, and at the heavy darkness bending over it like a curse, while our lamps made drips of light down the first two or three gloomy steps. Our bedrooms were on the ground floor, and stood opposite one another off a passage which led to a garden. Into mine Frank conducted me, and left me for his own.

The uneasy feeling which I have described did not go from me with him, and I felt a restlessness amounting to pain when left alone in my chamber. Efforts had evidently been made to render the room habitable, but there was a something antagonistic to sleep in every angle of its many crooked corners. I kicked chairs out of their prim order along the wall, and banged things about here and there; finally, thinking that a good night's rest was the best cure for an inexplicably disturbed frame of mind, I undressed as quickly as possible, and laid my head on my pillow under a canopy, like the wings of a gigantic bird of prey wheeling above me ready to pounce.

But I could not sleep. The wind grumbled in the chimney, and the boughs swished in the garden outside; and between these noises I thought I heard sounds coming from the interior of the old house, where all should have been still as the dead down in their vaults. I could not make out what these sounds were. Sometimes I thought I heard feet running about, sometimes I could have sworn there were double knocks, tremendous tantarararas at the great hall door. Sometimes I heard the clashing of dishes, the echo of voices calling, and the dragging about of furniture. Whilst I sat up in bed trying to account for these noises, my door suddenly flew open, a bright light streamed in from the passage without, and a powdered servant in an elaborate livery of antique pattern stood holding the handle of the door in his hand, and bowing low to me in the bed.

"Her ladyship, my mistress, desires your presence in the drawing-room, sir."

This was announced in the measured tone of a well-trained domestic. Then with another bow he retired, the door closed, and I was left in the dark to determine whether I had not suddenly awakened from a tantalising dream. In spite of my very wakeful sensations, I believe I should have endeavoured to convince myself that I had been sleeping, but then I perceived light shining under my door, and through the keyhole, from the passage. I got up, lit my lamp, and dressed myself as hastily as I was able.

I opened my door, and the passage down which a short time before I had almost groped my way, with my lamp blinking in the dense foggy darkness, was now illuminated with a light as bright as gas. I walked along it quickly, looking right and left to see whence the glare proceeded. Arriving at the hall, I found it also blazing with light, and filled with perfume. Groups of choice plants, heavy with blossoms, made it look like a garden. The mosaic floor was strewn with costly mats. Soft colours and gilding shone from the walls, and canvasses that had been black gave forth faces of men and women looking brightly from their burnished frames. Servants were running about, the dining-room and drawing-room doors were opening and shutting, and as I looked through each I saw vistas of light and colour, the moving of brilliant crowds, the waving of feathers, and glancing of brilliant dresses and uniforms. A festive hum reached me with a drowsy subdued sound, as if I were listening with stuffed ears. Standing aside by an orange tree, I gave up speculating on what this might be, and concentrated all my powers on observation.

Wheels were heard suddenly, and a resounding knock banged at the door till it seemed that the very rooks in the chimneys must be startled out of their nests. The door flew open, a flaming of lanterns was seen outside, and a dazzling lady came up the steps and swept into the hall. When she held up her cloth of silver train, I could see the diamonds that twinkled on her feet. Her bosom was covered with roses, and there was a red light in her eyes like the reflection from a hundred glowing fires. Her black hair went coiling about her head, and couched among the braids lay a jewel not unlike the head of a snake. She was flashing and glowing with gems and flowers. Her beauty and brilliance made me dizzy. Then came a faintness in the air, as if her breath had poisoned it. A whirl of storm came in with her, and rushed up the staircase like a moan. The plants shuddered and shed their blossoms, and all the lights grew dim a moment, then flared up again.

Now the drawing-room door was opened, and a gentleman came out with a young girl leaning on his arm. He was a fine-looking, middle-aged gentleman, with a mild countenance.

The girl was a slender creature, with golden hair and a pale face. She was dressed in pure white, with a large ruby like a drop of blood at her throat. They advanced together to receive the lady who had arrived. The gentleman offered his arm to the stranger, and the girl who was displaced for her fell back, and walked behind them with a downcast air. I felt irresistibly impelled to follow them, and passed with them into the drawing-room. Never had I mixed in a finer, gayer crowd. The costumes were rich and of an old-fashioned pattern. Dancing was going forward with spirit—minuets and country dances. The stately gentleman was evidently the host, and moved among the company, introducing the magnificent lady right and left. He led her to the head of the room presently, and they mixed in the dance. The arrogance of her manner and the fascination of her beauty were wonderful.

I cannot attempt to describe the strange manner in which I was in this company, and yet not of it. I seemed to view all I beheld through some fine and subtle medium. I saw clearly, yet I felt that it was not with my ordinary naked eyesight. I can compare it to nothing but looking at a scene through a piece of smoked or coloured glass. And just in the same way (as I have said before) all sounds seemed to reach me as if I were listening with ears imperfectly stuffed. No one present took any notice of me. I spoke to several, and they made no reply—did not even turn their eyes upon me, nor show in any way that they heard me. I planted myself straight in the way of a fine fellow in a general's uniform, but he, swerving neither to right or left by an inch, kept on his way, as though I were a streak of mist, and left me behind him. Everyone I touched eluded me somehow. Substantial as they all looked, I could not contrive to lay my hand on anything that felt like solid flesh. Two or three times I felt a momentary relief from the oppressive sensations which distracted me, when I firmly believed I saw Frank's head at some distance among the crowd, now in one room and now in another, and again in the conservatory, which was hung with lamps, and filled with people walking about among the flowers. But, whenever I approached, he had vanished. At last I came upon him, sitting by himself on a couch behind a curtain watching the dancers. I laid my hand upon his shoulder. Here was something substantial at last. He did not look up; he seemed aware neither of my touch nor my speech. I looked in his staring eyes, and found that he was sound asleep. I could not wake him.

Curiosity would not let me remain by his side. I again mixed with the crowd, and found the stately host still leading about the magnificent lady. No one seemed to notice that the golden-haired girl was sitting weeping in a corner; no one but the beauty in the silver train, who sometimes glanced at her contemptuously. Whilst I watched her distress a group came between me and her, and I wandered into another room, where, as though I had turned from one picture of her to look at another, I beheld her dancing gaily, in the full glee of "Sir Roger de Coverley", with a fine-looking youth, who was more plainly dressed than any other person in the room. Never was a better-matched pair to look at. Down the middle they danced, hand in hand, his face full of tenderness, hers beaming with joy, right and left, bowing and curtseying, parted and meeting again, smiling and whispering; but over the heads of smaller women there were the fierce eyes of the magnificent beauty scowling at them. Then again the crowd shifted around me, and this scene was lost.

For some time I could see no trace of the golden-haired girl in any of the rooms. I looked for her in vain, till at last I caught a glimpse of her standing smiling in a doorway with her finger lifted, beckoning. At whom? Could it be at me? Her eyes were fixed on mine. I hastened into the hall, and caught sight of her white dress passing up the wide black staircase from which I had shrunk some hours earlier. I followed her, she keeping some steps in advance. It was intensely dark, but by the gleaming of her gown I was able to trace her flying figure. Where we went I knew not, up how many stairs, down how many passages, till we arrived at a low-roofed large room with sloping roof and queer windows where there was a dim light, like the sanctuary light in a deserted church. Here, when I entered, the golden head was glimmering over something which I presently discerned to be a cradle wrapped round with white curtains, and with a few fresh flowers fastened up on the hood of it, as if to catch a baby's eye. The fair sweet face looked up at me with a glow of pride on it, smiling with happy dimples. The white hands unfolded the curtains, and stripped back the coverlet. Then, suddenly there went a rushing moan all round the weird room, that seemed like a gust of wind forcing in through the crannies, and shaking the jingling old windows in their sockets. The cradle was an empty one. The girl fell back with a look of horror on her pale face that I shall never forget, then, flinging her arms above her head, she dashed from the room.

I followed her as fast as I was able, but the wild white figure was too swift for me. I had lost her before I reached the bottom of the staircase. I searched for her, first in one room, then in another, neither could I see her foe (as I already believed to be), the lady of the silver train. At length I found myself in a small ante-room, where a lamp was expiring on the table. A window was open, close by it the golden-haired girl was lying sobbing in a chair, while the magnificent lady was bending over her as if soothingly, and offering her something to drink in a goblet. The moon was rising behind the two figures. The shuddering light of the lamp was flickering over the girl's bright head, the rich embossing of the golden cup, the lady's silver robes, and, I thought, the jewelled eyes of the serpent looked out from her bending head. As I watched, the girl raised her face and drank, then suddenly dashed the goblet away; while a cry such as I never heard but once, and shiver to remember, rose to the very roof of the old house, and the clear sharp word "*Poisoned!*" rang and reverberated from hall and chamber in a thousand echoes, like the clash of a peal of bells. The girl dashed herself from the open window, leaving the cry clamouring behind her. I heard the violent opening of doors and running of feet, but I waited for nothing more. Maddened by what I had witnessed, I would have felled the murderess, but she glided unhurt from under my vain blow. I sprang from the window after the wretched white figure. I saw her flying on before me with a speed I could not overtake.

I ran till I was dizzy. I called like a madman, and heard the owls croaking back to me. The moon grew huge and bright, the trees grew out before it like the bushy heads of giants, the river lay keen and shining like a long unsheathed sword, couching for deadly work among the rushes. The white figure shimmered and vanished, glittered brightly on before me, shimmered and vanished again, shimmered, staggered, fell, and disappeared in the river. Of what she was, phantom or reality, I thought not at the moment; she had the semblance of a human being going to destruction, and I had the frenzied impulse to save her. I rushed forward with one last effort, struck my foot against the root of a tree, and was dashed to the ground. I remember a crash, momentary pain and confusion; then nothing more.

When my senses returned, the red clouds of the dawn were shining in the river beside me. I arose to my feet, and found that, though much bruised, I was otherwise unhurt. I busied my mind in recalling the strange circumstances which had brought me to that place in the dead of the night. The recollection of all I had witnessed was vividly present to my mind. I took my way slowly to the house, almost expecting to see the marks of wheels and other indications of last night's revel, but the rank grass that covered the gravel was uncrushed, not a blade disturbed, not a stone displaced. I shook one of the drawing-room windows till I shook off the old rusty hasp inside, flung up the creaking sash, and entered. Where were the brilliant draperies and carpets, the soft gilding, the vases teeming with flowers, the thousand sweet odours of the night before? Not a trace of them; no, nor even a ragged cobweb swept away, nor a stiff chair moved an inch from its melancholy place, nor the face of a mirror relieved from one speck of its obscuring dust!

Coming back into the open air, I met the old man from the gate walking up one of the weedy paths. He eyed me meaningly from head to foot, but I gave him good-morrow cheerfully.

"You see I am poking about early," I said.

"I' faith, sir," said he, "an' ye look like a man that has been pokin' about *all night.*"

"How so?" said I.

"Why, ye see, sir," said he, "I'm used to 't, an' I can read it in yer face like prent. Some sees one thing an' some another, an' some only feels an' hears. The poor jintleman inside, *he* says nothin', but he has beautiful dhrames. An' for the Lord's sake, sir, take him out o' this, for I've seen him wandherin' about like a ghost himself in the heart o' the night, an' him that sound sleepin' that I couldn't wake him!"

At breakfast I said nothing to Frank of my strange adventures. He had rested well, he said, and boasted of his enchanting dreams. I asked him to describe them, when he grew perplexed and annoyed. He remembered nothing, but that his spirit had been delightfully entertained whilst his body reposed.

I now felt a curiosity to go through the old house, and was not surprised, on pushing open a door at the end of a remote mouldy passage, to enter the identical chamber into which I had followed the pale-faced girl when she beckoned me out of the drawing room. There were the low brooding roof and slanting walls, the short wide latticed windows to which the noonday sun was trying to pierce through a forest of leaves. The hangings rotting with age shook like dreary banners at the opening of the door, and there in the middle of the room was the cradle; only the curtains that had been white were blackened with dirt, and laced and overlaced with cobwebs. I parted the curtains, bringing down a shower of dust upon the floor, and saw lying upon the pillow, within, a child's tiny shoe, and a toy. I need not describe the rest of the house. It was vast and rambling, and, as far as furniture and decorations were concerned, the wreck of grandeur.

Having strange subject for meditation, I walked alone in the orchard that evening. This orchard sloped towards the river I have mentioned before. The trees were old and stunted, and the branches tangled overhead. The ripe apples were rolling in the long bleached grass. A row of taller trees, sycamores and chestnuts, straggled along by the river's edge, ferns and tall weeds grew round and amongst them, and between their trunks, and behind the rifts in the foliage, the water was seen to flow. Walking up and down one of the paths I alternately faced these trees and turned my back upon them. Once when coming towards them I chanced to lift my glance, started, drew my hands across my eyes, looked again, and finally stood still gazing in much astonishment. I saw distinctly the figure of a lady standing by one of the trees, bending low towards the grass. Her face was a little turned away, her dress a bluish-white, her mantle a dun-brown colour. She held a spade in her hand, and her foot was upon it, as if she were in the act of digging. I gazed at her for some time, vainly trying to guess at whom she might be, then I advanced towards her. As I approached, the outlines of her figure broke up and disappeared, and I found that she was only an illusion presented to me by the curious accidental grouping of the lines of two trees which had shaped the space between them into the semblance of the form I have described. A patch of the flowing water had been her robe, a piece of russet moorland her cloak. The spade was an awkward young shoot slanting up from the root of one of the trees. I stepped back and tried to piece her out again bit by bit, but could not succeed.

That night I did not feel at all inclined to return to my dismal chamber, and lie awaiting such another summons as I had received before. When Frank bade me goodnight, I heaped fresh coals on the fire, took down from the shelves a book, from which I lifted the dust in layers with my penknife, and, dragging an armchair close to the hearth, tried to make myself as comfortable as might be. I am a strong, robust man, very unimaginative, and little troubled with affections of the nerves, but I confess that my feelings were not enviable, sitting thus alone in that queer old house, with last night's strange pantomime still vividly present to my memory. In spite of my efforts at coolness, I was excited by the prospect of what yet might be in store for me before morning. But these feelings passed away as the night wore on, and I nodded asleep over my book.

I was startled by the sound of a brisk light step walking overhead. Wide awake at once, I sat up and listened. The ceiling was low, but I could not call to mind what room it was that lay above the library in which I sat. Presently I heard the same step upon the stairs, and the loud sharp rustling of a silk dress sweeping against the banisters. The step paused at the library door, and then there was silence. I got up, and with all the courage I could summon seized a light, and opened the door; but there was nothing in the hall but the usual heavy darkness and damp mouldy air. I confess I felt more uncomfortable at that moment than I had done at any time during the preceding night. All the visions that had then appeared to me had produced nothing like the horror of thus feeling a supernatural presence which my eyes were not permitted to behold.

I returned to the library, and passed the night there. Next day I sought for the room above it in which I had heard the footsteps, but could discover no entrance to any such room. Its windows, indeed, I counted from the outside, though they were so overgrown with ivy I could hardly discern them, but in the interior of the house I could find no door to the chamber. I asked Frank about it, but he knew and cared nothing on the subject; I asked the old man at the lodge, and he shook his head.

"Och!" he said, "don't ask about that room. The door's built up, and flesh and blood have no consarn wid it. It was *her own* room."

"Whose own?" I asked.

"Ould Lady Thunder's. An' whist, sir! *that's her grave!*"

"What do you mean?" I said. "Are you out of your mind?"

He laughed queerly, drew nearer, and lowered his voice. "Nobody has asked about the room these years but yourself," he said. "Nobody misses it goin' over the house. My grandfather was an old retainer o' the Thunder family, my father was in the service too, an' I was born myself before the ould lady died. Yon was her room, an' she left her eternal curse on her family if so be they didn't lave her coffin there. *She* wasn't goin' undher the ground to the worms. So there it was left, an' they built up the door. God love ye, sir, an' don't go near it. I wouldn't have told you, only I know ye've seen plenty about already, an' ye have the look o' one that'd be ferretin' things out, savin' yer presence."

He looked at me knowingly, but I gave him no information, only thanked him for putting me on my guard. I could scarcely credit what he told me about the room; but my curiosity was excited regarding it. I made up my mind that day to try and induce Frank to quit the place on the morrow. I felt more and more convinced that the atmosphere was not healthful for his mind, whatever it might be for his body. The sooner we left the spot the better for us both; but the remaining night which I had to pass there I resolved on devoting to the exploring of the walled-up chamber. What impelled me to this resolve I do not know. The undertaking was not a pleasant one, and I should hardly have ventured on it had I been forced to remain much longer at the Rath. But I knew there was little chance of sleep for me in that house, and I thought I might as well go and seek for my adventures as sit waiting for them to come for me, as I had done the night before. I felt a relish for my enterprise, and expected the night with satisfaction. I did not say anything of my intention either to Frank or the old man at the lodge. I did not want to make a fuss, and have my doings talked of all over the country. I may as well mention here that again, on this evening, when walking in the orchard, I saw the figure of the lady digging between the trees. And again I saw that this figure was an illusive appearance; that the water was her gown, and the moorland her cloak, and a willow in the distance her tresses.

As soon as the night was pretty far advanced, I placed a ladder against the window which was least covered over with the ivy, and mounted it, having provided myself with a dark lantern. The moon rose full behind some trees that stood like a black bank against the horizon, and glimmered on the panes as I ripped away branches and leaves with a knife, and shook the old crazy casement open. The sashes were rotten, and the fastenings easily gave way. I placed my lantern on a bench within, and was soon standing beside it in the chamber. The air was insufferably close and mouldy, and I flung the window open to the widest, and beat the bowering ivy still further back from about it, so as to let the fresh air of heaven blow into the place. I then took my lantern in hand, and began to look about me.

The room was vast and double; a velvet curtain hung between me and an inner chamber. The darkness was thick and irksome, and the scanty light of my lantern only tantalised me. My eyes fell on some tall spectral-looking candelabra furnished with wax candles, which, though black with age, still bore the marks of having been guttered by a draught that had blown on them fifty years ago. I lighted these; they burned up with a ghastly flickering, and the apartment, with its fittings, was revealed to me. These latter had been splendid in the days of their freshness: the appointments of the rest of the house were mean in comparison. The ceiling was painted with fine allegorical figures, also spaces of the walls between the dim mirrors and the sumptuous hangings of crimson velvet, with their tarnished golden tassels and fringes. The carpet still felt luxurious to the tread, and the dust could not altogether obliterate the elaborate fancy of its flowery design.

There were gorgeous cabinets laden with curiosities, wonderfully carved chairs, rare vases, and antique glasses of every description, under some of which lay little heaps of dust which had once no doubt been blooming flowers. There was a table laden with books of poetry and science, drawings and drawing materials, which showed that the occupant of the room had been a person of mind. There was also a writing-table scattered over with yellow papers, and a work-table at a window, on which lay reels, a thimble, and a piece of what had once been white muslin, but was now saffron colour, sewn with gold thread, a rusty needle sticking in it. This and the pen lying on the inkstand, the paper-knife between the leaves of a book, the loose sketches shaken out by the side of a portfolio, and the ashes of a fire on the wide mildewed hearth-place, all suggested that the owner of this retreat had been snatched from it without warning, and that whoever had thought proper to build up the doors, had also thought proper to touch nothing that had belonged to her.

Having surveyed all these things, I entered the inner room, which was a bedroom. The furniture of this was in keeping with that of the other chamber. I saw dimly a bed enveloped in lace, and a dressing-table fancifully garnished and draped. Here I espied more candelabra, and going forward to set the lights burning, I stumbled against something. I turned the blaze of my lantern on this something, and started with a sudden thrill of horror. It was a large stone coffin.

I own that I felt very strange for the next few minutes. When I had recovered from the shock, I set the wax-candles burning, and took a better survey of this odd burial-place. A wardrobe stood open, and I saw dresses hanging within. A gown lay upon a chair, as if just thrown off, and a pair of dainty slippers were beside it. The toilet-table looked as if it was only used yesterday, judging by the litter that covered it; hair-brushes lying this way and that way, essence-bottles with the stoppers out, paint pots uncovered, a ring here, a wreath of artificial flowers there, and in front of all that coffin, the tarnished Cupids that bore the mirror between their hands smirking down at it with a grim complacency.

On the corner of this table was a small golden salver, holding a plate of some black mouldered food, an antique decanter filled with wine, a glass, and a phial with some thick black liquid, uncorked. I felt weak and sick with the atmosphere of the place, and I seized the decanter, wiped the dust from it with my handkerchief, tasted, found that the wine was good, and drank a moderate draught. Immediately it was swallowed I felt a horrid giddiness, and sank upon the coffin. A raging pain was in my head and a sense of suffocation in my chest. After a few intolerable moments I felt better, but the heavy air pressed on me stiflingly, and I rushed from this inner room into the larger and outer chamber. Here a blast of cool air revived me, and I saw that the place was changed.

A dozen other candelabra besides those I had lighted were flaming round the walls, the hearth was all ruddy with a blazing fire, everything that had been dim was bright, the lustre had returned to the gilding, the flowers bloomed in the vases. A lady was sitting before the hearth in a low armchair. Her light loose gown swept about her on the carpet, her black hair fell round her to her knees, and into it her hands were thrust as she leaned her forehead upon them, and stared between them into the fire. I had scarcely time to observe her attitude when she turned her head quickly towards me, and I recognised the handsome face of the magnificent lady who had played such a sinister part in the strange scenes that had been enacted before me two nights ago. I saw something dark looming behind her chair, but I thought it was only her shadow thrown backward by the firelight.

She arose and came to meet me, and I recoiled from her. There was something horridly fixed and hollow in her gaze, and filmy in the stirring of her garments. The shadow, as she moved, grew more firm and distinct in outline, and followed her like a servant where she went.

She crossed half of the room, then beckoned me, and sat down at the writing-table. The shadow waited beside her, adjusted her paper, placed the ink-bottle near her and the pen between her fingers. I felt impelled to approach her, and to take my place at her left shoulder, so as to be able to see what she might write. The shadow stood motionless at her other hand. As I became accustomed to the shadow's presence he grew more visibly loathsome and hideous. He was quite distinct from the lady, and moved independently of her with long ugly limbs. She hesitated about beginning to write, and he made a wild gesture with his arm, which brought her hand quickly to the paper, and her pen began to move at once. I needed not to bend and scrutinise in order to read. Every word as it was formed flashed before me like a meteor.

"I am the spirit of Madeline, Lady Thunder, who lived and died in this house, and whose coffin stands in yonder room among the vanities in which I delighted. I am constrained to make my confession to you, John Thunder, who are the present owner of the estates of your family."

Here the hand trembled and stopped writing. But the shadow made a threatening gesture, and the hand fluttered on.

"I was beautiful, poor, and ambitious, and when I entered this house first on the night of a ball given by Sir Luke Thunder, I determined to become its mistress. His daughter, Mary Thunder, was the only obstacle in my way. She divined my intention, and stood between me and her father. She was a gentle, delicate girl, and no match for me. I pushed her aside, and became Lady Thunder. After that I hated her, and made her dread me. I had gained the object of my ambition, but I was jealous of the influence possessed by her over her father, and I revenged myself by crushing the joy out of her young life. In this I defeated my own purpose. She eloped with a young man who was devoted to her, though poor, and beneath her in station. Her father was indignant at first, and my malice was satisfied; but as time passed on I had no children, and she had a son, soon after whose birth her husband died. Then her father took her back to his heart, and the boy was his idol and heir."

Again the hand stopped writing, the ghostly head drooped, and the whole figure was convulsed. But the shadow gesticulated fiercely, and, cowering under its menace, the wretched spirit went on:

"I caused the child to be stolen away. I thought I had done it cunningly, but she tracked the crime home to me. She came and accused me of it, and in the desperation of my terror at discovery, I gave her poison to drink. She rushed from me and from the house in frenzy, and in her mortal anguish fell in the river. People thought she had gone mad from grief for her child, and committed suicide. Only I knew the horrible truth. Sorrow brought an illness upon her father, of which he died. Up to the day of his death he had search made for the child. Believing that it was alive, and must be found, he willed all his property to it, his rightful heir, and to its heirs for ever. I buried the deeds under a tree in the orchard, and forged a will, in which all was bequeathed to me during my lifetime. I enjoyed my state and grandeur till the day of my death, which came upon me miserably, and, after that, my husband's possessions went to a distant relation of his family. Nothing more was heard of the fate of the child who was stolen; but he lived and married, and his daughter now toils for her bread – his daughter, who is the rightful owner of all that is said to belong to you, John Thunder. I tell you this that you may devote yourself to the task of discovering the wronged girl, and giving up to her that which you are unlawfully possessed of. Under the thirteenth tree standing on the brink of the river at the foot of the orchard you will find buried the genuine will of Sir Luke Thunder. When you have found and read it, do justice, as you value your soul. In order that you may know the grandchild of Mary Thunder when you find her, you shall behold her in a vision—"

The last words grew dim before me; the lights faded away, and all the place was in darkness, except one spot on the opposite wall. On this spot the light glimmered softly, and against the brightness the outlines of a figure appeared, faintly at first, but, growing firm and distinct, became filled in and rounded at last to the perfect semblance of life. The figure was that of a young girl in a plain black dress, with a bright, happy face, and pale gold hair softly banded on her fair forehead. She might have been the twin-sister of the pale-faced girl whom I had seen bending over the cradle two nights ago; but her healthier, gladder, and prettier sister.

When I had gazed on her some moments, the vision faded away as it had come; the last vestige of the brightness died out upon the wall, and I found myself once more in total darkness. Stunned for a time by the sudden changes, I stood watching for the return of lights and figures; but in vain. By-and-by my eyes grew accustomed to the obscurity, and I saw the sky glimmering behind the little window which I had left open. I could soon discern the writing-table beside me, and possessed myself of the slips of loose paper which lay upon it. I then made my way to the window. The first streaks of dawn were in the sky as I descended my ladder, and I thanked God that I breathed the fresh morning air once more, and heard the cheering sound of the cocks crowing.

All thought of acting immediately upon last night's strange revelations, almost all memory of them, was for the time banished from my mind by the unexpected trouble of the next few days. That morning I found an alarming change in Frank. Feeling sure that he was going to be ill, I engaged a lodging in a cottage in the neighbourhood, whither we removed before nightfall, leaving the accursed Rath behind us. Before midnight he was in the delirium of a raging fever.

I thought it right to let his poor little *fiancée* know his state, and wrote to her, trying to alarm her no more than was necessary. On the evening of the third day after my letter went I was sitting by Frank's bedside, when an unusual bustle outside aroused my curiosity, and going into the cottage kitchen I saw a figure standing in the firelight which seemed a third appearance of that vision of the pale-faced golden-haired girl which was now thoroughly imprinted on my memory—a third, with all the woe of the first and all the beauty of the second. But this was a living, breathing apparition. She was throwing off her bonnet and shawl, and stood there at home in a moment in her plain black dress.

I drew my hand across my eyes to make sure that they did not deceive me. I had beheld so many supernatural visions lately that it seemed as though I could scarcely believe in the reality of anything till I had touched it.

"Oh, sir," said the visitor, "I am Mary Leonard, and are you poor Frank's friend? Oh, sir, we are all the world to one another, and I could not let him die without coming to see him!"

And here the poor little traveller burst into tears. I cheered her as well as I could, telling her that Frank would soon, I trusted, be out of all danger. She told me that she had thrown up her situation in order to come and nurse him. I said we had got a more experienced nurse than she could be, and then I gave her to the care of our landlady, a motherly country-woman. After that I went back to Frank's bedside, nor left it for long till he was convalescent. The fever had swept away all that strangeness in his manner which had afflicted me, and he was quite himself again.

There was a joyful meeting of the lovers. The more I saw of Mary Leonard's bright face the more thoroughly was I convinced that she was the living counterpart of the vision I had seen in the burial chamber. I made inquiries as to her birth, and her father's history, and found that she was indeed the grandchild of that Mary Thunder whose history had been so strangely related to me, and the rightful heiress of all those properties which for a few months only had been mine. Under the tree in the orchard, the thirteenth, and that by which I had seen the lady digging, were found the buried deeds which had been described to me. I made an immediate transfer of property, whereupon some others who thought they had a chance of being my heirs disputed the matter with me, and went to law. Thus the affair has gained publicity, and become a nine days' wonder. Many things have been in my favour, however: the proving of

Mary's birth and of Sir Luke's will, the identification of Lady Thunder's handwriting on the slips of paper which I had brought from the burial chamber; also other matters which a search in that chamber brought to light. I triumphed, and I now go abroad, leaving Frank and his Mary made happy by the possession of what could only have been a burden to me.

So the MS. ends. Major Thunder fell in battle a few years after the adventure it relates. Frank O'Brien's grandchildren hear of him with gratitude and awe. The Rath has been long since totally dismantled and left to go to ruin.

The Haunted Organist
of Hurly Burly

There had been a thunderstorm in the village of Hurly Burly. Every door was shut, every dog in his kennel, every rut and gutter a flowing river after the deluge of rain that had fallen. Up at the great house, a mile from the town, the rooks were calling to one another about the fright they had been in, the fawns in the deer-park were venturing their timid heads from behind the trunks of trees, and the old woman at the gate-lodge had risen from her knees, and was putting back her prayer-book on the shelf. In the garden, July roses, unwieldy with their full-blown richness, and saturated with rain, hung their heads heavily to the earth; others, already fallen, lay flat upon their blooming faces on the path, where Bess, Mistress Hurly's maid, would find them, when going on her morning quest of rose-leaves for her lady's pot-pourri. Ranks of white lilies, just brought to perfection by today's sun, lay dabbled in the mire of flooded mould. Tears ran down the amber cheeks of the plums on the south wall, and not a bee had ventured out of the hives, though the scent of the air was sweet enough to tempt the laziest drone. The sky was still lurid behind the boles of the upland oaks, but the birds had begun to dive in and out of the ivy that wrapped up the home of the Hurlys of Hurly Burly.

This thunderstorm took place more than half a century ago, and we must remember that Mistress Hurly was dressed in the fashion of that time as she crept out from behind the squire's chair, now that the lightning was over, and, with many nervous glances towards the window, sat down before her husband, the tea-urn, and the muffins. We can picture her fine lace cap, with its peachy ribbons, the frill on the hem of her cambric gown just touching her ankles, the embroidered clocks on her stockings, the rosettes on her shoes, but not so easily the lilac shade of her mild eyes, the satin skin, which still kept its delicate bloom, though wrinkled with advancing age, and the pale, sweet, puckered mouth, that time and sorrow had made angelic while trying vainly to deface its beauty.

The squire was as rugged as his wife was gentle, his skin as brown as hers was white, his grey hair as bristling as hers was glossed; the years had ploughed his face into ruts and channels; a bluff, choleric, noisy man he had been; but of late a dimness had come on his eyes, a hush on his loud voice, and a check on the spring of his hale step. He looked at his wife often, and very often she looked at him. She was not a tall woman, and he was only a head higher. They were a quaintly well-matched couple, despite their differences. She turned to you with nervous sharpness and revealed her tender voice and eye; he spoke and glanced roughly, but the turn of his head was courteous. Of late they fitted one another better than they had ever done in the heyday of their youthful love. A common sorrow had developed a singular likeness between them. In former years the cry from the wife had been, "Don't curb my son too much!" and from the husband, "You ruin the lad with softness." But now the idol that had stood between them was removed, and they saw each other better.

The room in which they sat was a pleasant, old-fashioned drawing-room, with a general spider-legged character about the fittings; spinet and guitar in their places, with a great deal of copied music beside them; carpet, tawny wreaths on pale blue; blue flutings on the walls, and faint gilding on the furniture. A huge urn, crammed with roses, in the open bay-window, through which came delicious airs from the garden, the twittering of birds settling to sleep in the ivy close by, and occasionally the pattering of a flight of rain-drops, swept to the ground as a bough bent in the breeze. The urn on the table was ancient silver, and the china rare. There was nothing in the room for luxurious ease of the body, but everything of delicate refinement for the eye.

There was a great hush all over Hurly Burly, except in the neighbourhood of the rooks. Every living thing had suffered from heat for the past month, and now, in common with all Nature, was receiving the boon of refreshed air in silent peace. The mistress and master of Hurly Burly shared the general spirit that was abroad, and were not talkative over their tea.

"Do you know," said Mistress Hurly, at last, "when I heard the first of the thunder beginning I thought it was—it was—"

The lady broke down, her lips trembling, and the peachy ribbons of her cap stirring with great agitation.

"Pshaw!" cried the old squire, making his cup suddenly ring upon the saucer, "we ought to have forgotten that. Nothing has been heard for three months."

At this moment a rolling sound struck upon the ears of both. The lady rose from her seat trembling, and folded her hands together, while the tea-urn flooded the tray.

"Nonsense, my love," said the squire; "that is the noise of wheels. Who can be arriving?"

"Who, indeed?" murmured the lady, reseating herself in agitation.

Presently pretty Bess of the rose-leaves appeared at the door in a flutter of blue ribbons.

"Please, madam, a lady has arrived, and says she is expected. She asked for her apartment, and I put her into the room that was got ready for Miss Calderwood. And she sends her respects to you, madam, and she'll be down with you presently."

The squire looked at his wife, and his wife looked at the squire.

"It is some mistake," murmured madam. "Some visitor for Calderwood or the Grange. It is very singular."

Hardly had she spoken when the door again opened, and the stranger appeared—a small creature, whether girl or woman it would be hard to say—dressed in a scanty black silk dress, her narrow shoulders covered with a white muslin pelerine. Her hair was swept up to the crown of her head, all but a little fringe hanging over her low forehead within an inch of her brows. Her face was brown and thin, eyes black and long, with blacker settings, mouth large, sweet, and melancholy. She was all head, mouth, and eyes; her nose and chin were nothing.

This visitor crossed the floor hastily, dropped a courtesy in the middle of the room, and approached the table, saying abruptly, with a soft Italian accent:

"Sir and madam, I am here. I am come to play your organ."

"The organ!" gasped Mistress Hurly.

"The organ!" stammered the squire.

"Yes, the organ," said the little stranger lady, playing on the back of a chair with her fingers, as if she felt notes under them. "It was but last week that the handsome signor, your son, came to my little house, where I have lived teaching music since my English father and my Italian mother and brothers and sisters died and left me so lonely."

Here the fingers left off drumming, and two great tears were brushed off, one from each eye with each hand, child's fashion. But the next moment the fingers were at work again, as if only whilst they were moving the tongue could speak.

"The noble signor, your son," said the little woman, looking trustfully from one to the other of the old couple, while a bright blush shone through her brown skin, "he often came to see me before that, always in the evening, when the sun was warm and yellow all through my little studio, and the music was swelling my heart, and I could play out grand with all my soul; then he used to come and say, 'Hurry, Little Lisa, and play better, better still. I have work for you to do by-and-by.' Sometimes he said, 'Brava!' and sometimes he said 'Eccellentissima!' but one night last week he came to me and said, 'It is enough. Will you swear to do my bidding, whatever it may be?'"

Here the black eyes fell.

"And I said, 'Yes.' And he said, 'Pack up your music, little Lisa, and go off to England to my English father and mother, who have an organ in their house which must be played upon. If they refuse to let you play, tell them I sent you, and they will give you leave. You must play all day, and you must get up in the night and play. You must never tire. You are my betrothed, and you have sworn to do my work.' I said, 'Shall I see you there, signor?' And he said, 'Yes, you shall see me there.' I said, 'I will keep my vow, signor.' And so, sir and madam, I am come."

The soft foreign voice left off talking, the fingers left off thrumming on the chair, and the little stranger gazed in dismay at her auditors, both pale with agitation.

"You are deceived. You make a mistake," said they in one breath.

"Our son——" began Mistress Hurly, but her mouth twitched, her voice broke, and she looked piteously towards her husband.

"Our son," said the squire, making an effort to conquer the quavering in his voice, "our son is long dead."

"Nay, nay," said the little foreigner. "If you have thought him dead have good cheer, dear sir and madam. He is alive; he is well, and strong, and handsome. But one, two, three, four, five" (on the fingers) "days ago he stood by my side."

"It is some strange mistake, some wonderful coincidence!" said the mistress and master of Hurly Burly.

"Let us take her to the gallery," murmured the mother of this son who was thus dead and alive. "There is yet light to see the pictures. She will not know his portrait."

The bewildered wife and husband led their strange visitor away to a long gloomy room at the west side of the house, where the faint gleams from the darkening sky still lingered on the portraits of the Hurly family.

"Doubtless he is like this," said the squire, pointing to a fair-haired young man with a mild face, a brother of his own who had been lost at sea.

But Lisa shook her head, and went softly on tiptoe from one picture to another, peering into the canvas, and still turning away troubled. But at last a shriek of delight startled the shadowy chamber.

"Ah, here he is! See, here he is, the noble signor, the beautiful signor, not half so handsome as he looked five days ago, when talking to poor little Lisa! Dear sir and madam, you are now content. Now take me to the organ, that I may commence to do his bidding at once."

The mistress of Hurly Burly clung fast by her husband's arm.

"How old are you, girl?" she said faintly.

"Eighteen," said the visitor, impatiently, moving towards the door.

"And my son has been dead for twenty years!" said his mother, and swooned on her husband's breast.

"Order the carriage at once," said Mistress Hurly, recovering from her swoon; "I will take her to Margaret Calderwood.

Margaret will tell her the story. Margaret will bring her to reason. No, not tomorrow; I cannot bear tomorrow, it is so far away. We must go tonight."

The little signora thought the old lady mad, but she put on her cloak again obediently, and took her seat beside Mistress Hurly in the Hurly family coach. The moon that looked in at them through the pane as they lumbered along was not whiter than the aged face of the squire's wife, whose dim faded eyes were fixed upon it in doubt and awe too great for tears or words. Lisa, too, from her corner gloated upon the moon, her black eyes shining with passionate dreams.

A carriage rolled away from the Calderwood door as the Hurly coach drew up at the steps. Margaret Calderwood had just returned from a dinner-party, and at the open door a splendid figure was standing, a tall woman dressed in brown velvet, the diamonds on her bosom glistening in the moonlight that revealed her, pouring, as it did, over the house from eaves to basement. Mistress Hurly fell into her outstretched arms with a groan, and the strong woman carried her aged friend, like a baby, into the house. Little Lisa was overlooked, and sat down contentedly on the threshold to gloat awhile longer on the moon, and to thrum imaginary sonatas on the doorstep.

There were tears and sobs in the dusk moonlit room into which Margaret Calderwood carried her friend. There was a long consultation, and then Margaret, having hushed away the grieving woman into some quiet corner, came forth to look for the little dark-faced stranger, who had arrived, so unwelcome, from beyond the seas, with such wild communication from the dead.

Up the grand staircase of handsome Calderwood the little woman followed the tall one into a large chamber where a lamp burned, showing Lisa, if she cared to see it, that this mansion of Calderwood was fitted with much greater luxury and richness than was that of Hurly Burly. The appointments of this room announced it the sanctum of a woman who depended for the interest of her life upon resources of intellect and taste. Lisa noticed nothing but a morsel of biscuit that was lying on a plate.

"May I have it?" she said eagerly. "It is so long since I have eaten. I am hungry."

Margaret Calderwood gazed at her with a sorrowful, motherly look, and, parting the fringing hair on her forehead, kissed her. Lisa, staring at her in wonder, returned the caress with ardour. Margaret's large fair shoulders, Madonna face, and yellow braided hair, excited a rapture within her. But when food was brought her, she flew to it and ate.

"It is better than I have ever eaten at home!" she said gratefully. And Margaret Calderwood murmured, "She is physically healthy, at least."

"And now, Lisa," said Margaret Calderwood, "come and tell me the whole history of the grand signor who sent you to England to play the organ."

Then Lisa crept in behind a chair, and her eyes began to burn and her fingers to thrum, and she repeated word for word her story as she had told it at Hurly Burly.

When she had finished, Margaret Calderwood began to pace up and down the floor with a very troubled face. Lisa watched her, fascinated, and, when she bade her listen to a story which she would relate to her, folded her restless hands together meekly, and listened.

"Twenty years ago, Lisa, Mr. and Mrs. Hurly had a son. He was handsome, like that portrait you saw in the gallery, and he had brilliant talents. He was idolized by his father and mother, and all who knew him felt obliged to love him. I was then a happy girl of twenty. I was an orphan, and Mrs. Hurly, who had been my mother's friend, was like a mother to me. I, too, was petted and caressed by all my friends, and

I was very wealthy; but I only valued admiration, riches—every good gift that fell to my share—just in proportion as they seemed of worth in the eyes of Lewis Hurly. I was his affianced wife, and I loved him well.

"All the fondness and pride that were lavished on him could not keep him from falling into evil ways, nor from becoming rapidly more and more abandoned to wickedness, till even those who loved him best despaired of seeing his reformation. I prayed him with tears, for my sake, if not for that of his grieving mother, to save himself before it was too late. But to my horror I found that my power was gone, my words did not even move him; he loved me no more. I tried to think that this was some fit of madness that would pass, and still clung to hope. At last his own mother forbade me to see him."

Here Margaret Calderwood paused, seemingly in bitter thought, but resumed:

"He and a party of his boon companions, named by themselves the 'Devil's Club', were in the habit of practicing all kinds of unholy pranks in the country. They had midnight carousings on the tombstones in the village graveyard; they carried away helpless old men and children, whom they tortured by making believe to bury them alive; they raised the dead and placed them sitting round the tombstones at a mock feast. On one occasion there was a very sad funeral from the village. The corpse was carried into the church, and prayers were read over the coffin, the chief mourner, the aged father of the dead man, standing weeping by. In the midst of this solemn scene the organ suddenly pealed forth a profane tune, and a number of voices shouted a drinking chorus. A groan of execration burst from the crowd, the clergyman turned pale and closed his book, and the old man, the father of the dead, climbed the altar steps, and raising his arms above his head, uttered a terrible curse. He cursed Lewis Hurly to all eternity, he cursed the organ he played, that it might be dumb henceforth, except under the fingers that had now profaned it, which, he prayed, might be forced to labour upon it till they stiffened in death. And the curse seemed to work, for the organ stood dumb in the church from that day, except when touched by Lewis Hurly.

"For a bravado he had the organ taken down and conveyed to his father's house, where he had it put up in the chamber where it now stands. It was also for a bravado that he played on it every day. But, by-and-by, the amount of time which he spent at it daily began to increase rapidly. We wondered long at this whim, as we called it, and his poor mother thanked God that he had set his heart upon an occupation which would keep him out of harm's way. I was the first to suspect that it was not his own will that kept him hammering at the organ so many laborious hours, while his boon companions tried vainly to draw him away. He used to lock himself up in the room with the organ, but one day I hid myself among the curtains, and saw him writhing on his seat, and heard him groaning as he strove to wrench his hands from the keys, to which they flew back like a needle to a magnet. It was soon plainly to be seen that he was an involuntary slave to the organ; but whether through a madness that had grown within himself, or by some supernatural doom, having its cause in the old man's curse, we did not dare to say. By-and-by there came a time when we were wakened out of our sleep at nights by the rolling of the organ. He wrought now night and day. Food and rest were denied him. His face got haggard, his beard grew long, his eyes started from their sockets. His body became wasted, and his cramped fingers like the claws of a bird. He groaned piteously as he stooped over his cruel toil. All save his mother and I were afraid to go near him. She, poor, tender woman, tried to put wine and food between his lips, while the tortured fingers crawled over the keys; but he only gnashed his teeth at her with curses, and she retreated from him in terror, to pray. At last, one dreadful hour, we found him a ghastly corpse on the ground before the organ.

"From that hour the organ was dumb to the touch of all human fingers. Many, unwilling to believe the story, made persevering endeavours to draw sound from it, in vain. But when the darkened empty room was locked up and left, we heard as loud as ever the well-known sounds humming and rolling through the walls. Night and day the tones of the organ boomed on as before. It seemed that the doom of the wretched man was not yet fulfilled, although his tortured body had been worn out in the terrible struggle to accomplish it. Even his own mother was afraid to go near the room then. So the time went on, and the curse of this perpetual music was not removed from the house. Servants refused to stay about the place. Visitors shunned it. The squire and his wife left their home for years, and returned; left it, and returned again, to find their ears still tortured and their hearts wrung by the unceasing persecution of terrible sounds. At last, but a few months ago, a holy man was found, who locked himself up in the cursed chamber for many days, praying and wrestling with the demon. After he came forth and went away the sounds ceased, and the organ was heard no more. Since then there has been peace in the house. And now, Lisa, your strange appearance and your strange story convince us that you are a victim of a ruse of the Evil One. Be warned in time, and place yourself under the protection of God, that you may be saved from the fearful influences that are at work upon you. Come—"

Margaret Calderwood turned to the corner where the stranger sat, as she had supposed, listening intently. Little Lisa was fast asleep, her hands spread before her as if she played an organ in her dreams.

Margaret took the soft brown face to her motherly breast, and kissed the swelling temples, too big with wonder and fancy.

"We will save you from a horrible fate!" she murmured, and carried the girl to bed.

In the morning Lisa was gone. Margaret Calderwood, coming early from her own chamber, went into the girl's room and found the bed empty.

"She is just such a wild thing," thought Margaret, "as would rush out at sunrise to hear the larks!" and she went forth to look for her in the meadows, behind the beech hedges, and in the home park. Mistress Hurly, from the breakfast-room window, saw Margaret Calderwood, large and fair in her white morning gown, coming down the garden-path between the rose bushes, with her fresh draperies dabbled by the dew, and a look of trouble on her calm face. Her quest had been unsuccessful. The little foreigner had vanished.

A second search after breakfast proved also fruitless, and towards evening the two women drove back to Hurly Burly together. There all was panic and distress. The squire sat in his study with the doors shut, and his hands over his ears. The servants, with pale faces, were huddled together in whispering groups. The haunted organ was pealing through the house as of old.

Margaret Calderwood hastened to the fatal chamber, and there, sure enough, was Lisa, perched upon the high seat before the organ, beating the keys with her small hands, her slight figure swaying, and the evening sunshine playing about her weird head. Sweet unearthly music she wrung from the groaning heart of the organ—wild melodies, mounting to rapturous heights and falling to mournful depths. She wandered from Mendelssohn to Mozart, and from Mozart to Beethoven. Margaret stood fascinated awhile by the ravishing beauty of the sounds she heard, but, rousing herself quickly, put her arms round the musician and forced her away from the chamber. Lisa returned next day, however, and was not so easily coaxed from her post again. Day after day she laboured at the organ, growing paler and thinner and more weird-looking as time went on.

"I work so hard," she said to Mrs. Hurly. "The signor, your son, is he pleased? Ask him to come and tell me himself if he is pleased."

Mistress Hurly got ill and took to her bed. The squire swore at the young foreign baggage, and roamed abroad. Margaret Calderwood was the only one who stood by to watch the fate of the little organist. The curse of the organ was upon Lisa; it spoke under her hand, and her hand was its slave.

At last she announced rapturously that she had had a visit from the brave signor, who had commended her industry, and urged her to work yet harder. After that she ceased to hold any communication with the living. Time after time Margaret Calderwood wrapped her arms about the frail thing, and carried her away by force, locking the door of the fatal chamber. But locking the chamber and burying the key were of no avail. The door stood open again, and Lisa was labouring on her perch.

One night, wakened from her sleep by the well-known humming and moaning of the organ, Margaret dressed hurriedly and hastened to the unholy room. Moonlight was pouring down the staircase and passages of Hurly Burly. It shone on the marble bust of the dead Lewis Hurly, that stood in the niche above his mother's sitting-room door. The organ room was full of it when Margaret pushed open the door and entered—full of the pale green moonlight from the window, mingled with another light, a dull lurid glare which seemed to centre round a dark shadow, like the figure of a man standing by the organ, and throwing out in fantastic relief the slight form of Lisa writhing, rather than swaying, back and forward, as if in agony. The sounds that came from the organ were broken and meaningless, as if the hands of the player lagged and stumbled on the keys. Between the intermittent chords low moaning cries broke from Lisa, and the dark figure bent towards her with menacing gestures. Trembling with the sickness of supernatural fear, yet strong of will, Margaret Calderwood crept forward within the lurid light, and was drawn into its influence. It grew and intensified upon her, it dazzled and blinded her at first; but presently, by a daring effort of will, she raised her eyes, and beheld Lisa's face convulsed with torture in the burning glare, and bending over her the figure and the features of Lewis Hurly! Smitten with horror, Margaret did not even then lose her presence of mind. She wound her strong arms around the wretched girl and dragged her from her seat and out of the influence of the lurid light, which immediately paled away and vanished. She carried her to her own bed, where Lisa lay, a wasted wreck, raving about the cruelty of the pitiless signor who would not see that she was labouring her best. Her poor cramped hands kept beating the coverlet, as though she were still at her agonising task.

Margaret Calderwood bathed her burning temples, and placed fresh flowers upon her pillow. She opened the blinds and windows, and let in the sweet morning air and sunshine, and then, looking up at the newly awakened sky with its fair promise of hope for the day, and down at the dewy fields, and afar off at the dark green woods with the purple mists still hovering about them, she prayed that a way might be shown her by which to put an end to this curse. She prayed for Lisa, and then, thinking that the girl rested somewhat, stole from the room. She thought that she had locked the door behind her.

She went downstairs with a pale, resolved face, and without consulting anyone, sent to the village for a bricklayer. Afterwards she sat by Mistress Hurly's bedside, and explained to her what was to be done. Presently she went to the door of Lisa's room, and hearing no sound, thought the girl slept, and stole away. By-and-by she went downstairs, and found that the bricklayer had arrived and already begun his task of building up the organ-room door. He was a swift workman, and the chamber was soon sealed safely with stone and mortar.

Having seen this work finished, Margaret Calderwood went and listened again at Lisa's door; and still hearing no sound, she returned, and took her seat at Mrs. Hurly's bedside once more. It was towards evening that she at last entered her room to assure herself of the comfort of Lisa's sleep. But the bed and room were empty. Lisa had disappeared.

Then the search began, upstairs and downstairs, in the garden, in the grounds, in the fields and meadows. No Lisa. Margaret Calderwood ordered the carriage and drove to Calderwood to see if the strange little Will-o'-the-wisp might have made her way there; then to the village, and to many other places in the neighbourhood which it was not possible she could have reached. She made inquiries everywhere; she pondered and puzzled over the matter. In the weak, suffering state that the girl was in, how far could she have crawled?

After two days' search, Margaret returned to Hurly Burly. She was sad and tired, and the evening was chill. She sat over the fire wrapped in her shawl when little Bess came to her, weeping behind her muslin apron.

"If you'd speak to Mistress Hurly about it, please, ma'am," she said. "I love her dearly, and it breaks my heart to go away, but the organ haven't done yet, ma'am, and I'm frightened out of my life, so I can't stay."

"Who has heard the organ, and when?" asked Margaret Calderwood, rising to her feet.

"Please, ma'am, I heard it the night you went away—the night after the door was built up!"

"And not since?"

"No, ma'am," hesitatingly, "not since. Hist! hark, ma'am! Is not that like the sound of it now?"

"No," said Margaret Calderwood; "it is only the wind." But pale as death she flew down the stairs and laid her ear to the yet damp mortar of the newly-built wall. All was silent. There was no sound but the monotonous sough of the wind in the trees outside. Then Margaret began to dash her soft shoulder against the strong wall, and to pick the mortar away with her white fingers, and to cry out for the bricklayer who had built up the door.

It was midnight, but the bricklayer left his bed in the village, and obeyed the summons to Hurly Burly. The pale woman stood by and watched him undo all his work of three days ago, and the servants gathered about in trembling groups, wondering what was to happen next.

What happened next was this: When an opening was made the man entered the room with a light, Margaret Calderwood and others following. A heap of something dark was lying on the ground at the foot of the organ. Many groans arose in the fatal chamber. Here was little Lisa dead!

When Mistress Hurly was able to move, the squire and his wife went to live in France, where they remained till their death. Hurly Burly was shut up and deserted for many years. Lately it has passed into new hands. The organ has been taken down and banished, and the room is a bed-chamber, more luxuriously furnished than any in the house. But no one sleeps in it twice.

Margaret was carried to her grave the other day a very aged woman.

The Mystery of Ora

There is something inexplicable in the story, but I tell you exactly as it happened.

Born to the expectation of wealth, certain casualties of fortune swept away my possessions at a blow. I was young enough to relish the thought of work, and for three years worked unremittingly, till my health began to feel the strain, and I resolved to take an open-air holiday. A friend who was to have accompanied me changed his mind at the last moment, and I set out alone.

I chose to visit the wildest parts of the west coast of Ireland, and was rewarded by the sight of some of the finest scenes I had ever beheld. Keeping the Atlantic on my right, losing sight of it for a time, and again finding it when some heathery ascent was gained, I walked for two or three days among lonely mountains, accepting hospitality from the poor occupants of the cabins I occasionally met with. It was fine August weather. All day the hill-peaks lay round me in blue ether; every evening the sun dyed them first purple, then blood-red, while the solitary slopes and vales became transfigured with a glory of colour quite indescribable. At night the solemn splendour that hung over this wilderness kept me awake, enchanted by the spells of a more mysterious moon than I had ever known elsewhere.

One morning I started to cross a ridge of mountain that separated me from the sea-shore, and was warned by the peasant whose breakfast of potatoes I had shared that I must travel a considerable distance before I could meet with shelter or food again.

"Ye'll see no roof till ye meet with the glass-house of ould Collum, the stargazer," he said. "An' ye needn't call there, for he spakes to no one, an' allows no man to darken his door. Keep always away to yer left, an' ye'll get to the village of Gurteen by nightfall."

"Who is this Collum, who allows no man to darken his door?" I asked.

"Nobody rightly knows what he is by this time, sir; but he was wanst a dacent man, only his head was light with always lookin' up at the stars. He built himself this glass-house, for all the world like a lighthouse; an' so far so good, for it did the turn of a lighthouse on them Eriff rocks, that'll tear a ship in ribbons like the teeth of a shark. An' there he did be porin' into books an' pryin' up at the heavens with his lamp burnin' at night; an' drawin' what he called horry-scopes, thinkin' he could tell a man's future an' know the saycrets of the Almighty. His wife was a nice poor thing, an' very good to travellers passing the way, an' his little girl was as gay and free as any other man's child; but somehow there's no good to be got of spyin' on the Creator; an' after his wife died he got queerer an' queerer, an' fairly shut himself up from his fellow-cratures; an' there he bes, an' there he remains. An' the daughter seems to have grown up as queer as himself, for she niver spakes to nobody, not these last three or four years, though she used to be so friendly."

"Well," I said, "I shall keep out of old Collum's way." And I started for my long day's walk.

I had walked a good many hours, and had crossed the steep ridge that separated me from the sea-board; had lain and rested at full-length in the heather, and gazed in delight at the magnificent view of the Atlantic, with its fringe of white low-lying serrated rocks, interrupted here and there by a group of black fortress-like cliffs, looking as though on their hither side they might have "casements opening on the foam of perilous seas" in these "faëry worlds forlorn". I had begun to descend the face of the mountain by a winding path when I became conscious of something moving at a little distance from me, and sheltering my eyes from the sun saw the figure of a woman against the strong light—a figure which came towards me with such a swift vehement movement that it seemed almost as if she had been shot from the blazing sky across my path. She put both her hands on my arm with a grasp of terror, and then stammering some incoherent words, extended one arm and pointed wildly to the sea—that serene ocean which a moment ago had looked to me like the very image of majestic peace, with its happy islets sparkling on its breast. What was there in that smiling, storm-forgetting ocean to excite the fear of any reasonable being? My first thought was that she was some poor maniac, whose all had gone down out there on some stormy night, and who had ever since haunted the scene of her shipwreck, calling for help. I could not see her features at first, so dark was she against the strong light that dazzled my eyes.

"What is the matter?" I asked. "What can I do for you?"

As I spoke I shifted my position so that I was in shade, while the light fell upon her; and then I saw that she was no madwoman, but a very beautiful girl, with a face full of strong character and vivid intelligence. The look in her eyes was the sane appeal of one human creature to another for protection; the white fear on her lips was a rational fear. The firm gracious lines of her young countenance suggested that no mere cowardly impulse had caused her to seize my arm with that agonised grasp.

As she stood gazing at me, with that transfixed look of terror and appeal, I saw how very beautiful she was, with the sunlight pouring round her and almost through her. Her glowing hair, which I had thought black, had flashed into the warmest auburn, and lay in sunny masses on her shoulders; her eyes, deep grey and heavily fringed, glowed from her pale face with a splendour I had never seen in eyes before. She was poorly and singularly dressed in a faded calico gown, and an old straw hat, tied down with a scarlet handkerchief; but even as she stood nothing could be more perfect than the artistic beauty of colour and form which she presented to my astonished eyes. Almost unconsciously I noticed this, for all my mind was engaged with the expectation of what she had to tell me, with the awe of that look of living imploring anguish, and the wonder as to what that message could be which she seemed to be bringing me from the ocean.

As she did not speak I repeated my question: "What is the matter? Tell me, I beg, what I can do to help you?"

Her eyes slowly loosened their gaze from my face, her arm fell to her side, a slight shudder passed over her, and she turned away.

"Nothing." She almost whispered the word, and moved a step from me.

"That is nonsense," I said, placing myself in her path. "Pardon me; but you are in some trouble—in some danger, and you thought I could save you from it, or, at least, help you. Let me try. Let me know how I can serve you."

"I cannot tell you," she murmured, and then raised her eyes again to mine with another wild look full of unutterable meaning. Behind her gaze there seemed to lie a lonely trouble, which peered out from its prison-house and asked for human sympathy, but was crossed and driven back by a cloud of unearthly fear. I thought so weird a look had never passed from one living creature to another.

I felt puzzled. So sure was I of the reality of her forlorn anguish that I could not think of passing on and leaving her to be the victim of whatever calamity threatened her under the shadow of this lonely mountain. And I felt, by an instinct, that the womanly weakness within her was clinging to me for protection in spite of the steadfast denial of her words.

"I am a stranger," I said, "and you are afraid to trust me; but I give you my word I am an honourable man—I will not take advantage of anything you may tell me."

Her lips quivered, and she glanced at me wistfully. She looked so young—so piteous! I took her passive hand firmly in mine, and said again: "Trust me."

"I do, I could," she faltered; "but oh! it is not that. It must never be told. I dare not speak."

She turned slowly round, and her eyes went fearfully out to the sea, wavered towards the cliffs, and lit on a glittering point among them; then she snatched her fingers from mine with a wail of terror, and, dropping on her knees before me, hid her face in her hands and wept.

I waited till her agony had spent itself, and then I raised her up gently and tried to reason with her. But it was all in vain. No confidence would pass her lips. She became every moment firmer, colder, more controlled. All her weakness seemed to have been washed away by her tears; and yet the calm despair on her soft face, bringing out its strongest lines of character, somehow touched me more than any complaint could have done.

"I thank you deeply," she said. "You would have helped me if you could. Go your way now, and I will go mine."

"I will at least bring you to your home," I said. "Where do you live?"

"There," she said, pointing to the glittering point on the rocks.

I shaded my eyes and looked keenly through the sunlight, and suddenly it flashed upon me that yon glitter came from "Old Collum's glass-house", and that this was his daughter.

"Is your father's name Collum?" I asked.

A sudden change passed over her—I knew not what—like an electric thrill.

"That is his name."

"And he lives at yonder observatory?"

"It is our home," she replied after a pause.

"Let me accompany you," I said.

"No one comes there; he—he does not make anyone welcome. I beg you will not mind me; I am accustomed to roam about alone."

"I have walked a long way," I said, after a few moments' reflection, "and I am tired and hungry. I hope you will not forbid my throwing myself on your father's hospitality for a few hours. I cannot reach the nearest village before nightfall."

This clever appeal of mine had its effect. She no longer urged me to leave her, though a painful embarrassment hung upon her. Under other circumstances delicacy would have forced me to relieve her from this, but I had made up my mind to leave no means untried to help her. I had a strong suspicion that old Collum was cruel to his child, and that she feared to let a stranger witness his ill-conduct. I determined to discover for myself, if I could, what sort of life he forced her to lead. We descended the mountain silently together, and, crossing a difficult passage of rocks, arrived at old Collum's house.

It was a curious old grey weather-beaten building, wedged into and sheltered by the cliffs, and looking as if in some early age it might have been carved out of their grim masses. The observatory was a much newer erection—a round tower with a glass chamber at the top, looking like a lighthouse to warn mariners from these dangerous rocks. The house was of two storeys—three rooms below and three above, and we ascended a narrow spiral stair to the higher chambers. My companion led the way to an apartment in the front—a dimly-lighted gloomy place, with two small windows set high in the wall, from which nothing could be seen but two square spaces of ocean. The interior of this room showed how very ancient the building must be, and it had, in fact, been built as a hermitage by monks in an early century. The stone walls, made without mortar, had never been plastered, and the rough dark edges of the stones had been polished and smoothed by time. Upon them hung a map of the world, one or two sea-charts, a compass, a great old-fash-ioned clock of foreign workmanship, ticking the time loudly, and a few pieces of ancient Irish armour and ornament dug out of a neighbouring bog. The floor was paved with stones, worn into hollows here and there, and skins of animals were strewn over it. The fire-place was a smoke-blackened alcove, and across it, sheltering its wide nakedness, the skin of a seal was hung, fixed in its place by an ancient skein, or knife, of curious workmanship. On the rude hearth-stone lay the red embers of a peat fire; and though an August sun was glowing in the heavens, yet fire did not seem out of place in the chill of this vault-like dwelling.

As we entered my companion cast a hurried glance into the room, and seemed relieved to find it unoccupied. She threw off her hat, and opening a cupboard began to prepare the table for the meal which I had begged of her. All her movements were graceful and lady-like, and her beauty seemed to take a new character as she made her simple housewifely arrangements. Excitement and exaltation were gone from her manner, wildness and brilliance from her looks. No longer glorified by the sun-light, her hair had ceased to flash with gold, and had darkened to blackness in the shadows of the room. Her down-cast eyes expressed only a gentle care for my comfort, and, as I watched her with increasing interest, a faint colour came and went in her face.

I took up a curious old drinking-cup of gold which she had placed on the table. On it was engraved the word "Ora", and I asked her what it meant.

"It is my name," she said. "The cup was found not far from here, and my father put my name upon it."

Now when she said this there was wonder in my mind, not that she bore so strange and original a name, but because the words "my father" were pronounced in a tone of such mournful and compassionate lovingness as to startle away all my preconceived notions as to the reason of her unhappiness.

"Perhaps, if not wicked, he is mad," I thought, "and she is afraid of having him taken away from her."

As I pondered this thought with my eyes fixed on the door, it opened, and a sallow withered face appeared, set with two dull black eyes, which fastened in blank astonishment on my face. "Collum, the madman!" was my mental exclamation on beholding this vision; but as the door opened farther, and a figure was added to the face, I saw that the intruder was a woman.

Ora turned to her, and raising her hands, talked to her on her fingers; then, as the old creature began to make up the fire, said to me:

"She is deaf and dumb, but a faithful soul, and all the servant we have. She goes our messages, fetches our provisions, and does little things which I cannot do myself."

"A strange household," I reflected: "an aged madman, a deaf and dumb crone, and this beautiful, living, vigorous creature! Outside, the wilderness of mountain and ocean. What a place—what company for Ora on winter nights!"

I said aloud: "And you, and she, and your father, are really the only dwellers in this lonely spot?"

She glanced up quickly, and a shudder of agitation passed over her, such as I had seen before. She did not reply for a few seconds, and then she said in a low pained voice:

"There are only three of us."

A most distressing feeling came over me—a conviction that the girl was answering me with a wary reserve, veiling her meaning so that, while she did not speak absolute untruth, she resolutely kept something hidden from me. Everything about her persuaded me that this was done against her will. Her eyes expressed a candid nature; her manner trusted me, except at moments when my words jarred on the secret chord of anguish. Some terrible dread made her treat me at such moments as an enemy.

I sat at table, and she waited upon me, serving me with an anxious care which made me feel ashamed of the pretence which had thrown me on her hospitality as a hungry man. I had little appetite, but, like Geraint, felt longing in me ever more "to stoop and kiss the tender little thumb that crossed the platter as she laid it down". My meal over I felt that she would expect me to depart; and as I ate I pondered as to how I could contrive to remain in old Collum's dwelling.

I was resolved not to go without making his acquaintance—yet how was I to force myself into the old man's presence? Even as the thought passed through my mind my question was answered. The door opened, and the master of this strange domicile appeared.

My first thought was that I found him much younger, keener, more vigorous and wide-awake than I had expected. Despite his long white hair, beard, and eye-brows, I saw at once that he was not a very old man; even his manner of opening the door, and the step with which he entered the room, gave one the idea of physical strength in its prime. There was no droop of the dotard about his features or figure—no dreamy absent look of the stargazer in his fierce black eyes—no lines of abstracted thought upon his cunning brow. As he entered the room, not expecting to see me, I saw him just as he was—in all his reality; and I felt at once that had he known I was there he would have presented a different appearance. I seemed to know this by instinct, as one does sometimes divine certain things, by a sudden flash of intelligence, in the first moment of meeting with a fellow creature.

As he stood in the doorway, looking at me with rage in his eyes, I saw his soul unveiled; the next moment—how or why I knew not—I beheld (my gaze having never been withdrawn from his face) a different being. The tension of his figure had slackened; the lines of his face lengthened and weakened; the shaggy grey brows veiled the languid eyes; the forehead had assumed the look of the forehead of a visionary. He flung himself on a seat, and said feebly:

"Excuse me, sir; but I did not know that our poor dwelling was honoured by the presence of a guest. Ora, my dear, you ought to have told me."

Ora was behind me, and so intent was I upon watching the strange being before me that I did not look to see how she had taken this address. Besides, something warned me that it would be better to notice her as little as possible in her father's presence. Striving to overcome the extreme repugnance I felt to my host, I said:

"It is I who ought to apologise for my intrusion, but"—here it seemed to me that I felt the thrill that quivered through Ora standing behind me—"but finding myself a complete stranger in need of rest and food in this lonely region, I ventured to throw myself on your daughter's hospitality. I am afraid, indeed, I forced myself upon her kindness."

"You are welcome, sir," he said; "welcome to all we have to give. We live out of the world, and have little to offer to those who are accustomed to better things."

His civil speech seemed to clear difficulties from my path, only to put greater ones in my way. That this wily man had, as well as his daughter, a secret to guard, was an established fact in my mind. That cruelty to her was not the whole of it I felt sure. Whether his civility was a proof that he feared, or did not fear, detection by me, I could not at the moment decide, but put the question away for after consideration, along with another fact which I had noted without weighing what its value might be. The man spoke with a foreign accent, and with a manner which suggested that English was not familiar to him, and had been learnt late in life. He was of foreign workmanship, as surely as was the quaint old clock that ticked so loudly over the ragged fire-place.

As I talked to my host I studied the name on my drinking-cup more frequently than his countenance. Something warned me that he would not endure anything like scrutiny; at the same time, I felt that I was undergoing a searching examination from the keen cruel eyes half hidden under their drooping eye-lids.

"You are an Englishman, I suppose?" he said.

"Yes."

"And have never been in this country before?"

"Never."

"And in all probability what you see of it in this holiday will be enough for you. You will hardly come back."

This was said with an affectation of carelessness which would have imposed upon me had suspicion not been aroused within me.

"Nothing is more unlikely than my return."

As I said this my conscience smote me, for I already felt that I could never more be entirely indifferent to the country which held Ora. The answer pleased him, however. There was a certain relief in his voice which I felt, and this encouraged me to make a bold stroke towards attaining my own purpose.

"I am going to make a request," I said, "which I hope you will not think impertinent. This bit of coast scenery is so beautiful that I feel a great longing to explore it further. I could not do so unless you will be so very good as to allow me to return here in the evening, and give me shelter for the night. I am well aware there is no dwelling in the direction I would take, and my health is not good enough for sleeping out of doors."

I prolonged my speech after my request was made to give him time to prepare his answer; and I forbore to raise my eyes to his so that he might have a moment to quench whatever light of ire my audacity might happen to call into them. There was a slight pause, which told me my precaution had not been an unnecessary one, but when I looked up his face was placid and bland.

"You are welcome," he said, "to what poor accommodation we can offer. Ora, let a room be prepared for this gentleman."

I thanked him, and took up my hat to go upon the excursion I had so newly designed. My host also rose and prepared to leave the room with me.

"The old owl must go back to his nest," he said, with an attempt at pleasantry. "I am a dabbler in astronomy, an observer of the stars, and my days pass in making calculations. My observatory is my home. When I entered the room some time ago I was irritated beyond measure by a problem, the solution of which still eludes me. A little society has soothed me, and I shall return to my labours refreshed."

This speech convinced me more than ever that he was an impostor. Not only had his words of information about himself a false ring in them, but his apology for his appearance in the moment when he had stood unveiled before me revealed a depth of consciousness which was betrayed by the effort to hide it. If anything had been wanting to complete the impression made by him upon me, it would have been supplied by the evil look which he turned upon Ora as he left the room. This look he, of course, intended to be unseen by me, and I was thankful my interception of it was unperceived. It was a significant look of warning, and contained a threat.

He went to his observatory, and I took my way over the jagged rocks along the sea-shore, thinking deeply over all I had seen and heard.

It seemed to me that I had to sum up a number of contradictory evidences. That old Collum was not the visionary nor the star-gazer which public report and his own representations declared him to be, was to me past doubting. That he had some heavy stake in this lower world, and was playing a part to win it, I believed, upon the strength of my own observations. Yet what object was to be gained by a life of such entire seclusion as his? The wildest ideas occurred to my imagination as to the possibilities of leading a criminal life in this wilderness; and were rejected almost as quickly as they took shape in my mind. His well-known inhospitality forbade the supposition that he could be a waylayer of travellers; and besides, had he been a murderer, Ora would not have stayed by him. She was free to roam where she pleased, and could as easily have escaped to the nearest town as she could have climbed the mountain upon which she had met me. It was more likely that he might be a forger, and an undertaker of secret journeys into the world and back again to his den. Could her knowledge of his evil life account for her conduct? I thought it might, and yet, having granted this, I still felt that there was a mystery behind which I could not unravel. One moment I felt convinced that Ora hated and feared him, and that it was from him she would have appealed to me for protection; the next I remembered the accent of love with which she dwelt on the words "my father", uttering them in a tone that was crossed by neither shame nor terror. And another point remained in my thoughts, though I knew not what conclusion I could draw from it. The man was of a foreign nation. I believed that he was not a European. True, my informant might have overlooked this fact when giving me his slight sketch of the unloved recluse, but from his name I had concluded he was an Irishman. "Collum" I had supposed must be a namesake of St. Columba; but, of course, it might as easily be a corruption of some difficult Eastern word. From an Irish mother Ora might have inherited her wonderful grey eyes and tender bloom, together with a mind and heart as beautiful as her exquisite face.

The only result my cogitations produced was a feeling of satisfaction that I was going to pass one night at least under old Collum's roof. I acknowledged to myself that there seemed very little likelihood of my being thus enabled to make any discovery; but the vague hope, that during the next twenty-four hours I might find some faint clue to Ora's mystery, cheered me in spite of reasonable probability. I felt no pang of conscience at the thought of playing the spy upon my host. The one fact that remained clear on my mind regarding him was that he was a criminal who ought to be detected, whose existence blighted the life of the innocent girl who had the misfortune to be his child. And then my thoughts wandered from him and rested exclusively on Ora.

As I lay upon the rocks with my hands clasped behind my head, gazing out to sea, my eyes roamed over the numerous islands that lay scattered on its bosom for miles towards the horizon. Some looked large enough to support life, others were mere clusters of rocks; yonder one was gleaming like an emerald in the sun and seeming to invite the tired traveller to a sea-girt paradise, while over there another lowered, making a spot of sinister gloom on the smiling ocean. One that bore this latter character had a peculiar fascination for me. Its jagged rocks were like cruel teeth; it showed no cheerful fleck of green even when the sun touched it a moment and fled away. It seemed always in shadow, and had a fierce gloom in its aspect that made one shiver. "All that enter here leave hope behind," I murmured, looking at it, and fancying it might well be the home of despairing spirits.

Birds were wheeling above it, and as I watched them, now black in the shadow and not white in the sun, I fell into a sort of dream—slumbering lightly, yet never losing the consciousness of where I was. I thought I heard the birds talking loudly to each other, and they talked of Ora.

"Pluck her out of yonder dungeon," said one, "and carry her far over the sea!"

"I cannot," said the other; "she is chained to the rock. Her father has chained her, and she will not tell."

I started out of this dream to find that the sun had set, and I resolved to return at once to the observatory. When I arrived the door of the house lay open, and I went in without seeing anyone, and ascended the winding stone stair which did not creak under the foot.

In the room where I had left her Ora was sitting alone. Outside it was still daylight, but in this gloomy chamber with its small high windows dusk had long set in, and a small lamp burned on the table, throwing a heavier darkness into the corners around. The young girl sat by the lamp, poring intently into a book. The lamp-light fell full on her face; and on that beautiful face was such a look of horror as it froze my blood to see. So absorbed was she that she did not perceive my approach, and I paused involuntarily, pained at seeing her suffering soul thus laid bare before me once more. Surprise deprived me for some moments of the power of speech. To find Ora a student was about the last thing I should have expected. To see her buried in a study which, from the expression on her face, I could not but fancy in some way connected with the woe of her life, was a still greater cause for amazement. Could she be conning some task which had been set her; or striving to forget in the pages of a book moments of terror which were only just past? But no; as she read, all her mind, all her being, were engaged with what the book conveyed to her; and as the moments passed, that fearful indescribable look grew and grew on her face, till at last she raised her eyes and fixed them on vacancy with a gaze which seemed to threaten madness.

I could not bear it any longer.

"Ora!" I cried, touching her shoulder, "for Heaven's sake tell me what horrible thing you are looking at!"

She started violently, and let the book fall, put out her arm to bar my taking it up, and then sank back in her chair exhausted by conflicting feeling. As before I seemed to feel her passionate desire to confide in me—a desire struggling in the chains of her deadly fear. I gently put away her hand and took up the book.

"Let me look at it?" I said. "What harm can it do? You shall not tell me anything but what you please. The book can surely betray no secrets."

She bent her head, and I opened the book. It was old and worn, the cover worm-eaten, the pages yellow and brown with time. The type was so strange, that at first sight it seemed to be written in a foreign language; but as my eye became accustomed to it I was able to read.

It was a book on necromancy, treating of the power of the Evil One, and of the mighty and terrible things he enabled those to do who leagued themselves with him and played into his hands. It was written with a certain force of imagination and diction, and, apparently, a thoroughness of faith in what it set forth, which was calculated to exercise an almost fiendish influence over a sensitive and delicate mind, and of which even the strongest and most sceptical reader must for a moment feel the spell. As I turned page after page, and gradually mastered the entire drift of the book, I asked myself could it be that all the terrors of the supernatural had been brought to bear upon Ora's imagination, and that the fears which bound her were of this extraordinary nature?

"You do not believe a word of all this terrible nonsense?" I said smiling, as I closed the uncanny volume, which seemed almost to smell of brimstone.

She gazed at me with a look of amazement, in which there was for a second a gleam of something like relief.

"Ah," she said, "you talk like that because you are ignorant. You are not so well educated as I am. See here!"

She drew back a curtain that covered some rows of rude book-shelves, all filled with volumes looking like fit companions of the book on the table.

"Look over these," said Ora, "and you will see that my instruction has not been neglected."

I did look through them, and found them the most extraordinary assemblage of compositions that ever were brought together for the bewilderment of human creatures. There were several long treatises on astrology, dream-like mystical books full of fascination; then came augury, the knowledge of signs and omens; necromancy, witchcraft, and vividly detailed information regarding leagues with the person of Satan which powerfully underlay all the movements of the world.

"If these and these only have been your school-books," I reflected, "Heaven help you, poor Ora!"

I thought of a lonely childhood and youth passed in this wilderness of rock and ocean, of winters which were probably all one long howling storm, and asked myself how the poor girl had preserved her senses, fed upon such teaching as this.

"Are these books your father's?" I asked, hardly able to contain my indignation against the wretch who had so poisoned her mind.

"Some of them," she answered, with a quiver of the lip; "those on astrology."

"And who gave you the others?"

She trembled, cast at me the wild look she had given me on the mountain, and threw up her hands in a defensive attitude.

"Don't!" she said hoarsely. "Don't ask me questions. If I answer them I shall have to hate you for evermore."

She then turned quickly towards the wall, and leaning against it, hid her face between her hands.

The words, the movement, gave me a thrill of gladness.

"Ora," I said, "you must never hate me. Nay, listen to me. If you can love me instead, I will take you away out of this miserable life, with its secret dread of—Heaven only knows what! As my wife you shall have every happiness that a loving heart can procure for you. And I shall ask you no questions. If ever a moment comes when you feel that you can confide in me, dear, I shall trust that then you will speak."

I drew away her hands from her face, and she looked at me with a bewildered blush of surprise.

"You?" she stammered. "You would marry me?"

"Is that so very unreasonable?"

Her face became gradually glorified by a look of such radiant joy as showed me for an instant what happiness might make of her; but it quickly faded away: the joy went out like light in a gust of wind, the blush was replaced by an ashen pallor.

"Oh, why has this come to me," she murmured with quivering lips, "only to be found impossible, only to deepen my misery?"

"Why impossible, Ora?"

"That I cannot tell you. If I were to tell you it would bring such ruin as you could not bear to hurl upon me."

Having said this her old reticent calm descended upon her like armour; she withdrew herself from me, went over to the table, and taking up the book she had been reading replaced it on the shelf with its companions, drawing the curtain across, as if to prevent any return to the discussion of the subject of her studies. Then she stood silently waiting as if expecting me to leave her.

"You had better go to your room," she said gently. "He—he will be displeased if he finds you here with me."

I obeyed her desire at once, fearing to bring down a tyrant's wrath upon that tender head.

The room assigned to me was small, but its window was well placed, being in the gable of the house, and thus commanding a noble view both of the inland, with its mountains, and the island-strewn sea. True, it was rather out of reach, and at an inconvenient height—so that an effort must be made if one wanted to enjoy the outer world through its medium. It would seem, indeed, as if the windows of this house had been planned with a view to shutting out the perpetual sight of the ocean which was so near. Had the builder foreseen that future dwellers within the walls might find the companionship of the great ocean monotonously intolerable? Whether or not, the blindness, so to speak, of the house, and the bold and peering inquisitiveness of the observatory close by, struck me as contrasting with each other curiously.

I extinguished my light and threw myself on the bed, but felt that I was not likely to sleep. My mind flew back over all the events of the day, and I could scarcely believe that I was the same person who had parted from his peasant-entertainer in the morning, saying: "I will take care to avoid old Collum's dwelling." I felt as if years must have elapsed since the time when I had never seen Ora, since the moment when I saw her darting to meet me upon the mountain, as if the sun had cast her upon my path. Since I had beheld that light of love and joy in her face, I resolved that nothing would induce me to give up the hope of making her my wife—no impenetrable mystery should daunt me; no terror, natural or supernatural, should be allowed to wrench her away from me. At the same time, I must be careful not to persecute her. Ignorant as I was of the cause of her sorrow and fear I must be content to wait patiently; if necessary, to watch over her from a distance. Time, which unveils wonders, would be certain to unravel the mystery in which Ora was entangled.

As the night advanced I became more and more fevered with tantalising thoughts and vain speculations, and at last, just as the first faint indications of approaching dawn appeared, I left my bed, and with some difficulty established myself in such a position at the window as enabled me to have a view of all the landscape beauties below. I looked sheer down into a bed of rocks, which went like jagged steps to the sea; and beyond this foreground lay the ocean, with its islands dimly discernible in the misty daybreak. One by one the darkness gave up its hidden treasures, and allowed them to creep under the mysterious grey veil of the morning.

"The sun will come," I said to myself. "The sun will come; and presently how beautiful all this will be!"

I was trying to persuade myself that so would the clouds and mysteries of Ora's life dissolve away, when a slight sound immediately below startled me, a sound no greater than the flutter of a bird's wing, but sufficient in the intense stillness to make me look to see whence it proceeded. And I did look, and beheld a sight which surprised me: Ora gliding over the rocks like a spirit, stopping to look about anxiously as if afraid of being observed, and then hurrying on towards the sea. A shawl was round about her head and shoulders, and she carried a basket on her arm. She was clearly going on a journey, and was making towards the verge of the cliffs. Was it possible her household duties could take her away to a distance at this extraordinary hour? And whither could she be going by water?

I lost sight of her for a few moments as she disappeared among the rocks, but soon a little boat shot out from beyond them, and Ora was in it, rowing away from the land with all her might.

Outward, still outward, I saw her darting like an impatient bird over the calm sea in the still grey dawn. The wildest thoughts came into my mind. Was she fleeing away frantically, trying to escape from all her troubles at once: from the mystery of her home, from my love and the discoveries it might impel me to make, from every difficulty that beset her? And whither? Had she any plan; or did she in her ignorance hope vaguely that she might reach by chance some goal of safety, touch with her little hunted feet some shore of peace, where, unknown and unquestioned, she might loosen the cords of misery by forgetting her own identity?

Suddenly my crazy thoughts were rebuked, and I saw that she had a simple and definite purpose in her voyage. She was making for one of the islands out yonder that were creeping one by one out of the shadows of the night. It was that particular isle of gloomy and fantastic shape and expression on which yesterday the sun had refused to shine, and over which the birds had talked and wheeled in my dream. She neared it, touched it; I saw her moor the boat, and vanish among the rocks of the island shore.

After an interval of half an hour she reappeared, and presently I saw her coming, small and scarcely visible as she and her skiff were in the distance, and looking, as she plied her oars, like some dark sea-bird on the wing. Landing where she had embarked, she returned along the rocks, with swift glances of alarm cast on all sides, and sped like a frightened dove into the shadows of the house.

I mused long over this secret expedition of Ora's. Her evident fear of being seen, and the fact that she bore with her a well-filled basket, which she carried carefully, bringing back the same basket empty, forbade me to suppose that she could have gone to fetch any simple produce of the island for household purposes. Whose observation had she feared? Not mine, for she never once glanced towards my window. Had she waited till her father had left his observatory, and might be supposed to be asleep, before she stole forth in her solitary adventure? And if not, what was the purpose of her visit to the island? I felt assured that some human creature's need had drawn her to the secret expedition; she was supplying sustenance to that creature unknown to and in defiance of her father. I did not guess these facts; I divined them at once; and the knowledge gave an added pang to my mind.

Who was the person lingering in retreat upon that gloomy island? Why did he stay there? If it were a man who had thus secured the devotion of a woman like Ora, why did he not free himself and her? Why did he not step into her boat, and escape with her into the safety of the vastness of the world? I wearied myself with asking questions, with indulging my indignation against this cowardly protégé of Ora's, who was content to lie by and let her suffer, till my reasoning powers returned, and I remembered that I knew nothing of the facts of the case.

On leaving my tiny apartment I found breakfast ready for me in the sitting-room, and Ora waited upon me as she had done the day before. She looked unnaturally pale, and there were dark circles round her eyes that told a tale of suffering. She was in her most impenetrable mood, and I scarcely ventured to speak to her. Whilst I was at breakfast old Collum came into the room, and though he kept up an appearance of civility in his manner towards me, yet I felt that my hour had come, and that I must go. He had bestowed his society upon me in order that he might see me out of the house. There, in his presence, I was obliged to say good-bye to Ora, and left the place accompanied by the man, who walked with me a mile along the shore.

I arrived at Gurteen in the evening, but found it impossible either to stay there or go farther away from old Collum's observatory. The knowledge of Ora's lonely trouble held me like a cord, and the thought of that gloomy island, with Ora's little boat speeding towards it, haunted me wherever I turned. The over-whelming desire to know more of the mystery I had left behind me so deprived me of the power of pursuing any other idea, so ignored all difficulties in the way of discovery, that I gave up battling with it, and resolved to spend the remaining time at my disposal in hovering near the spot which I had quitted in the morning. Having rested a few hours at the village inn, I set out again in the twilight to walk back again the way I had come, without having any positive purpose in so doing, and drawn only by the craving to see whether Ora's little boat would again be on the water in the still grey hour that lies between the night and the dawn.

At a certain distance from Ora's home I found a cave in the rocks in which I could rest, with my eyes on that line across the sea from the house by the observatory to the gloomy island. A faint moonlight illuminated the track as

I began my watch; but it soon vanished with its shadows, and in the pale obscurity that followed I saw the thing I had expected to see—Ora's small barque on its solitary voyage. She went and came as on the preceding night, and in the sunrise there came a vivid light across my mind. I remembered that when Ora met me on the mountain she had pointed towards the sea: she had indicated the very island which she now visited by night. I had felt that she was bringing me some message from the ocean, but afterwards I had forgotten this striking impression made by her gesture in the first moment of her appearance. Now the first and the last seemed to join and close the circle of my speculations: the beginning and end of Ora's mystery was centred in the island.

I passed the succeeding hours in making up my mind to a certain course, as a man does who finds he must steer between two inevitable dangers. I felt that I must run the risk of incurring Ora's hate—of overwhelming her with that ruin of which she had spoken. I must dare even that in the effort to save her. And yet what ruin could overtake her innocent youth? There was no shadow of guilt on her face, and I would never allow her to involve herself in the well-deserved ruin of others. With all this reasoning I came to my conclusion, and made my arrangements with a sense of the deepest pain. I was going to win Ora, or to lose her. At all events I would set her free.

Retracing my steps to the village, I hired a boat and set out to row myself to the mysterious island. Rowing through the red sunset on my strange quest, like a man in a dream, I touched the lonely shores of my desire; and mooring my boat in a creek on the seaward side of the isle, I slowly went my way to discover what it might support or contain. Nothing did I find but rocks and heather and a sprinkling of grass. There was no sign of any human habitation, no evidence of life except the occasional cries of the gulls and curlews. What brought Ora here, night after night, in the silent hours? Did she come to feed the birds, or did some supernatural power compel her to a rendezvous with unquiet spirits? I smiled as this latter thought passed through my mind; but truly there was something witch-like in the shapes and expressions of the surrounding rocks as twilight came on—something uncanny and eerie in the sough of the breeze through the heather, and the lapping and murmuring of the great calm ocean that girdled me. All through the hours of the night I walked the island, listening, watching, straining every faculty in the intensity of my vigil; sometimes starting in pursuit of an imaginary figure, which seemed to climb the rocks on before me or to dart across the streaks of the moonlight, but always finding that fancy had taken advantage of some accidental form of an inanimate thing to deceive me.

At last the moon set, and that scared wakening look came over the sea which means the dawn; and the pale hours brought Ora. When I saw her coming my heart misgave me as to the wisdom of my adventure. I was going to spy on her, to hunt her down, to possess myself by stratagem of her secret. The fear of her hate unmanned me; but with a strong effort I thrust aside such weakness. I had come here, not to injure, but to save her.

She landed close to where I lay hidden. She moored her boat and climbed the cliffs, and I followed her. So safe from observation did she consider herself, that she never once thought of turning her head, and I kept near her easily till I saw her suddenly stoop, and apparently vanish into the rock.

Coming to the spot where she had disappeared, I found an opening in the stone, and, stooping as she had stooped, followed her down an irregular winding passage, which led to a subterranean cave. I had completely lost her, and groped my way in the dark; but after some minutes I heard the murmur of voices, and presently saw the glimmer of a light. Approaching this light, I came to an opening into a wider cave, on the floor of which a lamp burned, throwing a dreary light on two figures that clung together in the gloom of the subterranean solitude. One of them was Ora, who had flung herself on the neck of the man, who was evidently a prisoner in this natural dungeon.

A dizziness seized me, and for some moments made me forget myself and my purpose in coming to the place. I stood as if stunned. I had no idea of listening; but across the cloud that had descended on my mind I heard the low tones of Ora's voice murmuring with infinite tenderness:

"Oh, father! oh, father! oh, poor, poor, father!"

The soft words, with their despairing, caressing monotony, flowed into my ear and into my brain like a river of light. Her father was here. The other was an impostor. Foul work had been done. I thought no more of displeasing Ora, but stepped into the cave.

At sight of me Ora uttered a low cry of anguish that I can never forget, and wound her arms round the old man (who looked to me like an aged, etherealised likeness of the knave in the observatory), as if she would protect him from some deadly harm. The man's eyes were turned in the direction where I stood with a look of ghastly expectancy rather than fear, while Ora's were fixed on his face with that sort of gaze we turn on the dying when the parting soul is hovering upon their lips. So they remained, locked in each other's arms, waiting as if for a sword to pierce them.

"Ora," I said, "what does this mean? I am come to save, not to hurt you."

She answered not a word—she did not seem to hear me; but the old man spoke to me at last, slowly and awfully, as if from the verge of another world.

"Sir," he said, "you mean well; but, unknown to yourself, you have brought ruin to me. This is the hour of death."

His head sank on his breast, and again I endured a long silence, which seemed hardly broken by our breathing. I bore it as long as I could, and then I spoke again.

"Let me beg you to listen to me," I said. "There is no one on this island, save ourselves. I am a friend; I can help. Why do you associate me with death?"

With a long sigh the strange old man raised his head, and said:

"I know not why I am still here to answer you; but believe that I do not blame you. You are but the voice of fate. Yes, Ora; I read it long ago in the stars, and it was folly of me to think to escape my doom. Stranger, the blow that I expect will not fall from any human hand, but none the less will it fall. You are innocent of all purpose against my life, yet your discovery of me here is the signal for my death. Suffer me to pass my last moments in peace with my child."

Hearing this speech, I made up my mind that the poor old man was mad; and resolving to humour him, I retreated to some distance, and gave no sign of my existence for a considerable time. After an interval which seemed to me an age, I at last spoke again.

"Pardon me," I said; "but you perceive that from some cause or other the event you expect has been delayed. Will you not make use of the time thus given you to think of your daughter? The doom you speak of does not include her."

"I have no fear for her. I have read her happy fate in the stars. Freed from me, the last of her troubles will be over. Friend, I feel a desire to tell you my story. If time be granted to me, I will do it."

I hailed the words with joy, and prepared to listen.

"I am an astrologer. For long years I lived among the stars, and they revealed to me secrets not known to men who walk the earth looking downward. I knew early that misfortune would cloud the latter days of my life; but the nature of the misfortune was not made clear to me. When I lost my dear wife, I thought for a time that the trouble I was forewarned of had come; but my child grew up loving me, and happiness returned to my heart. I kept a close sharp watch for the shadow that was sure to descend upon me, and yet it took me unawares.

"The winters on this coast are terrible, and on wild nights I used to place a light in my observatory as an assistance to mariners. More than once I was thanked by sailors who had seen 'Collum's light' in time. Yet through this charity to others came my doom.

"One terrible night I became convinced that a ship was wrecking somewhere among these dangerous islands, and I got out my boat, and pushed my way to sea as well as I could, hoping to be the means of saving life. I heard cries, but could not reach the spot, nor discover the direction whence they came. I was driven on this island a little before dawn, and then the voices had ceased, and I felt that all was over without my having been able to afford any help.

"Pacing along the shore, my foot struck against something unusual, and by the first glimmer of daybreak I perceived that it was a chest which had evidently been washed up from the wreck. Examining it carefully, I found that it was locked and sealed. 'Some valuable cargo, no doubt,' I thought, and wondered what I should do with it. As I bent over it I suddenly became aware that someone was near, and looking up, saw a young man standing beside me. I stared at him in amazement, for he was neither wet nor ill, nor did he bear any trace of having lately striven with death on the sea. He had a gentlemanly, thoughtful air, and returned my gaze with a half anxious, half confiding look.

" 'What can I do for you?' I asked, as soon as surprise would allow me to speak.

" 'Guard this,' he said, pointing to what lay at our feet. 'It is all I possess. Save it from my enemy. Keep it for me till I come for it.'

" 'Where shall I put it?' I asked, and stooped to try if I could lift it.

"When I looked up again the young man had disappeared. A second ago my eyes had been fixed upon his; now I was alone. I gazed up and down the lonely shore, and climbed the rocks and called. Nothing human met my eyes. No one replied to me. Then I remembered something strange about the young man's manner—the sudden way he had come upon me, the unsuitableness of his dress, the impossibility of his having found his way to the island without a boat; and I knew that I had seen an apparition.

"The peculiar, anxious, confiding expression of his eyes remained upon my memory, and I vowed I would be true to his trust. I buried the chest where no man save myself can ever find it, and then I went to look for my boat.

"As I went I met with another startling object. Right across my path lay what seemed the corpse of a man, cold and blue—a drowned waif from the wreck. He bore no likeness to the young man who had so strangely appeared and disappeared, but was short and dark, with sallow skin and Egyptian features. Why did I touch him? But had I left him lying there, the stars had been untrue in their reckoning.

"I knelt beside him, restored him to life, and brought him home. Ora and I nursed him. He was ill some time, and I amused his sick-bed with stories of my way of life, and told him many of the wonderful things the stars had revealed to me. He listened with great interest, and seemed grateful and friendly. I gave him all my confidence, and in an unlucky moment related to him the strange occurrence of my vision on the island, and of the burying of the coffer I had found. He told me he was the master of the merchant vessel that had been lost, and was concerned about all details of the wreck.

"As soon as he was able to move he asked me to accompany him to this island that he might search for such scraps of his property as the winds and waves might cast upon its shore. He picked up several things which he claimed as his own; and after he had ceased to find anything from day to day, he still kept urging me to visit this place with him. I soon perceived that he was trying to discover whereabouts I had buried the coffer.

"Finding that I would not betray myself, he at last spoke to me plainly—told me that the coffer was his, that my pretence of having seen an apparition was a trick to deprive him of his property, and that he meant to have it, whether I would or not. Now I knew that the thing I had hidden was neither his nor mine, and so I resisted him.

"We were here in this cave, where he had beguiled me on pretence of looking for waifs from the wreck. Suddenly he struck me on the head, and I fell senseless. When I recovered consciousness I was here as you see me, chained by the ankles in this miserable hole.

"My enemy then returned to my house, took advantage of a certain likeness to myself in his features to personate me, and established himself in my place. From time to time he visits me here, trying to persuade me to give up the coffer; but that I will never do till the owner comes for it."

Here the poor creature paused, and I said quickly:

"All this I fully understand. You have been treated most foully. But why, in Heaven's name, did you not suffer your daughter to make known your state. Why do you shrink from me and talk of death in the very moment when I have come to deliver you?"

Now up to this time the old man had told his story with the air of an intelligent person; but the moment I asked the latter question a gleam of insanity seemed to dart across his brain.

"Why?" he asked excitedly. "Because my enemy is a wizard, a magician; he is in league with the Evil One, who holds me in his claw, ready to strike death into my veins the instant my case is made known to any creature. Have I not seen Satan in the long black hours pacing up and down yonder passage, and stopping to look in and gloat over his prey? But he could not touch me so long as we—as Ora and I—kept the secret to ourselves. I would not speak, and I would not suffer her to betray me. And so I baffled them."

There was a ring of triumph in the poor old creature's voice as he said this, and he patted Ora's head almost gleefully, where she leaned with her face buried in his breast.

I said to myself that he was mad—driven quite mad by this solitary confinement, and his unhappy daughter had never discovered it.

"How could you believe," I said, "that your enemy had this supernatural power over your life?"

"How can I believe that the sun shines?" he asked gravely. "He comes here and sits beside me, and tells me of his dealings with Satan. He has lived, and will live, hundreds of years, though Lucifer, who does his will now, is bound to get him at last. You might not have believed him, but I knew better. The secrets of the stars had taught me many things."

"But tell me," I said, "if this terrible person has Satan for his servant, why does he not find him the coffer without your assistance?"

"It is a fault in the plan," answered the old man dreamily. "When Satan tried to see, he was baffled by an angel's wing. I cannot explain it to you, but I know it well enough myself."

"The angel was your daughter, then. Through her I have come here. Now listen to me, old man. Why were you not brave enough to die, and let your child go free?"

He hung his head on his breast, and fondled Ora's hair.

"You are right, sir," he said. "I will die, and she shall go free. Let the blow fall; it is due ere this."

"Then, if you are ready, I will strike off your chain, and let Satan do his worst."

Ora started up as I drew near, and seized my arm.

"Ora," I whispered, "poor child! do you not see that affliction has crazed your father's brain? Do not you also be mad, but let me deal with him."

I examined the chain, and found, as I expected, that it was eaten with rust. It was probably something belonging to the shipwrecked vessel which had come ashore. I laid a rusty link upon a large sharp stone, and lifting another stone, as heavy a one as I could raise, to a considerable height, let it fall upon the iron. As I raised my arms to do this, the lamplight fell full on my face, and I glanced at the poor old maniac, who, with folded arms, awaited his imaginary doom. In that instant, as the stone dropped, a terrible cry broke from his lips, and he fell back with a groan, just as his chain split asunder.

"He is dead. We have murdered him!" moaned Ora, falling on her knees beside him.

"No, he is not dead!" I exclaimed joyfully; for I had feared that the shock of expectation might have really deprived him of life. I poured brandy down his throat, and after a time he revived.

"The apparition," he muttered; "he has the face of the apparition. Ora, where is the young man who met me that morning on the shore?"

"He is wandering," I said to Ora. "Do not be afraid."

"I am not wandering," said the old man. "What I saw I saw. Reach me the lamp."

He raised the light to my face, and looked at me with a solemn, awful look.

"It was you who met me on the shore," he said; "you who gave the coffer in charge to me."

When the wretch whom I had known as "old Collum" saw us coming in our boat from the island, he escaped on the instant, and we saw him no more. The police made efforts to track him, but in vain.

I told you that there was a strange point about this story, and so, when the haze of folly and madness had been cleared away, there still remains something in it that is inexplicable. Urged by the poor old dotard whom I had rescued, I went with him to unearth the coffer which it had cost him so much to guard. It proved to be my own property, and its contents restored to me the fortune I had lost.

Its loss in a ship that went down at sea had been the cause of the reverses which I mentioned at the beginning of my tale. A comparison of dates proved, if proof were necessary, that the vessel wrecked off the island was the same that had borne my heritage across the sea. The incident of the apparition I do not attempt to account for. That, on the morning after the wreck, I had spoken with him on the shore, and committed my property to his care, was firmly believed by poor old Collum up to the moment of his death—a moment not far distant from that which saw his rescue from the cave.

Wrought upon so long by a knave on the one side, and a visionary and madman on the other, it was long ere Ora's tender imagination recovered from the morbid state into which it had been thrown by her terrible experiences. But time and change cleared away all clouds from her mind; while the energy and devotion that characterised the wild mountain girl remain to my beautiful wife.

A Strange Love Story

I.

At the foot of a certain street in Innsbruck, right above the famous gold-roofed house, rise the purple walls of the Alps, mountain walls so apparently straight and perpendicular that they seem, according to the mood of the spectator, either to block the way to heaven, or to lead to it by difficult ascent. On a summer day a young girl, who knew all the accessible paths of yonder great stepping-stones to the skies, walked down this street in Innsbruck with her back to the golden roof, and all the purple glory of the Alps behind and above her. She wore a high-crowned Alpine hat with a silver tassel, and a costume of hunting-green cloth. Her face was round and fair, and her crystal-clear eyes had a look of unusually vivid intelligence. The hair which curled softly and crisply round her temples, and was plaited in thick masses at the back of her head, was of that fairness which is almost white, and is seldom seen except on very young children. Her features were small and softly moulded, and something very like the light of genius was shining from her countenance.

She walked on with a bright pre-occupied look, as if something beautiful which other people could not see had caught her eye and fixed her attention; and then suddenly turned in at the open door of that curious church, where a strange company of bronze men and women occupy for ever the centre of the nave.

The only living creatures in the church were a few old women in furry head-dresses, at prayer, and a very young man who was standing with folded arms studying the bronze statues. The girl made no noise crossing the threshold of the door, but the moment she entered, the young man started electrically and turned to see her coming towards him, a glow of delight on his face as if the sun had suddenly shone out upon it. She came quietly and stood by his side.

"Have you gazed enough for today?" she asked with a twinkle of glee in her eyes. "Come, Max, it is your work I want to see, not these."

Max shook his head, but caught the little hand she placed imperatively on his, and followed her out of the shadows of the church into the dazzling summer street, where the sun was glittering on the eaves of the gold-roofed house, and making the huge Alpine walls behind it take a richer purple than before.

Max was a tall youth, with a square-browed dreamy face, full of a kind of rugged beauty. His eyes had not the vivid light that glanced from the eyes of the girl, but they were full of dreams of glories to come, burning with a latent fire destined yet to give its share towards the warming and lighting up of the world. He led the way into a small house at the corner of the street, and up a staircase into a bare room littered with clay, with half-formed images and casts, and where an unfinished statue in clay stood near the window. From the face of this statue he withdrew the cloth, and gazed discontentedly at the face of the creature he had made, a nymph graceful and lovely, with the features of the girl at his side.

"It is you, Hilda," he said, "but without your soul in the eyes. When you are not here it is like you, but when I see your face beside it—"

"Nonsense! you do not want a likeness of me," said Hilda; "you want an ideal being! It only wants a little tenderness, dear Max. May I touch it?"

Max nodded, and Hilda's little fingers passed over the clay with a few delicate touches, while a curious look of intellectual power grew on her face and changed its character for a moment. After a few minutes she withdrew behind Max, and peeped over his shoulder to see the effect of what she had done.

Max drew a deep breath and stared in amazement at the change which had been wrought. The statue which had been coldly perfect seemed to breathe.

"Your power is supernatural," he murmured; "the work is now divine."

"You are dreaming," said Hilda, laughing. "All the divinity in it is your own; I but drew forth what you had left slightly veiled."

Max shook his head. "I am too much the artist," he said, "not to recognise your gift. But I am not jealous of you, Hilda. With you by my side what may I not hope to accomplish?"

Hilda laid a hand on his arm and looked into his face with joyful eyes.

"Do not make me vain," she said; "but if cooking your dinner and keeping your house in order, doing all that woman can do to make your home happy, and your difficult upward path a little easier; if all that helps you to accomplish great things, then, indeed, I shall feel you are the better for me."

Max took both her hands in his, and looked down into her eyes with a wondering, worshipping gaze, which troubled almost as much as it delighted her. As if she feared what might be his next change of mood she turned away her head, and said gaily:

"Come with me now at once. You promised to take a holiday today. Let us be off to the mountains, and leave this nymph to her solitary thoughts."

He put on his hat mechanically, and again followed her whither she would lead him. They went out of the town, and took the road to the mountains. The world was exquisite, and Max shook himself out of his dreams to enjoy it. Hilda prattled to him between bursts of laughter about all that had occurred at home, up yonder in the blue, since his last visit there; what droll things the children had said; what a pleasant dance there had been at a neighbour's wedding; how Lisbeth had burned a hole in her new dress, and all the trouble there had been to get it nicely mended. People going down to the town passed them, and said, "That is Max Edelstein and his betrothed, Hilda."

"What a pity they cannot get married at once," said one.

"They could if they liked, for Hilda has a nice little penny which her father left her."

"It is a pity when people are too clever, you see. Nothing will suit them but going to Rome."

"They will be a long time saving to go to Rome. Who is there to buy his sculptures in Innsbruck? Better if he had been content with wood-carving like so many of his friends."

The lovers reached the nook of the mountains in which their village nestled. Lisbeth, Hilda's sister-in-law, was expecting them, and had made a little feast. A table was spread under a tree at her door, and a troop of little sun-burnt children came dashing out to meet Hilda and her Max.

Lisbeth, a good-humoured, brown-eyed woman, with a flame-coloured hand-kerchief twisted round her head, and wearing her holiday jacket of black, embroidered with threads of gold, came out of the house with a baby on one arm, and placed some fruit upon the table. The wooden chálet was set deep in a cool green cave of boughs, on a platform of rock, and under it and opposite to it, lay a dazzling landscape of purple crag, teeming golden valley, and woods of all the richest hues of green. Up a pathway, seemingly made for goats, our lovers climbed, and were welcomed by the motherly Lisbeth. The master of the little home, Lisbeth's husband, Hilda's brother, wood-carver, hunter, and tiller of the earth, now appeared, and the elders partook of Lisbeth's feast in the shade, while the little sun-burnt children capered and danced in the sun.

Max cast off the cloud of dreaminess that often wrapped him up, and talked to Fritz about the crops and the hunts, and all that was interesting in the mountaineer's life. The artist disappeared for the time, and Max was merely a stalwart youth of the mountains, with an unusually picturesque and intellectual face. Hilda took the baby in her arms, and laughter and prattle made the time fly fast, till Lisbeth said:

"Ah, Max, have you seen the present that Hilda has given me? She has modelled my little dead Lisa, so that I think I have her back."

"Will not you show it to me, Hilda?"

"Yes, if you please; but it is only interesting to Lisbeth, dear Max."

The day passed and evening came. Songs were sung, and Hilda accompanied them on the zither. Throwing away her silver-tasselled hat she put on an apron, prepared the supper, and carried it out under the trees. Her fair head gleamed in the sunset as she went and came, and as a wave of warm light suddenly fell across her face and hands, Max thought she looked like a ministering angel descended to wait upon them. After supper some young friends came from a little distance, and Fritz strummed the zither while a dance was held on a bit of green close by. Hilda danced with as much glee as any of the children. The moon shone out, the children pulled Hilda's hair about, till it flowed around her like a gold and silver mantle, and Max would not have it put up again, and danced with her while it streamed about her shoulders.

"Hilda looks beautiful tonight, does she not?" said one of her friends. "What a pity she will marry that melancholy Max!"

"He is not melancholy now when he is dancing."

"He is always strange, and full of fancies. I would rather marry a man who could make a joke."

The dancing was over, the neighbours had gone home, and Max was asking again to see Hilda's model of Lisbeth's little angel Lisa. Hilda led him up the narrow stairs, and into her own small chamber, where one of the ruddy little dancers of an hour ago was asleep in her bed. It was a tiny brown room, where almost the only decoration was the oblong moonlit picture of pine and crag framed by the open window. Hilda struck a light and lit a hand-lamp, and discovered on a bench the model of the child who was dead.

Max folded his arms, and gazed at it long and critically.

"Hilda!" he said, "I wonder if you know what a genius you possess!"

"Through my love for you I have learned to dabble in clay; that is all," said Hilda. "I have no genius, and I do not want it."

"About this going to Rome. It is you who ought to go, not I."

"Max! where are your wits? I wish there was money enough for two, then we could go together. But as there is not, why I must wait till you can afford to send for me."

"What I mean is this, Hilda," said Max, with the sadness in his eyes deepening to gloom. "You have a distinct genius of your own, and I ought not to be so selfish as to absorb you into my own life and work. You have money to take yourself to Rome, and there you ought to go. Marriage for you will be the ruin of an artist."

"Not the ruin of you, I hope."

"No, of yourself."

"Then let me be ruined, dear Max, and let the world lose what it will never have possessed. I belong to you, and not either to art or to the world."

"I am a traitor to art to listen to you."

"Then be a traitor. I love you better as a traitor."

Max shook his head, and gloomily withdrew the hand which Hilda had touched with her own.

Hilda uttered a sudden cry, and snatching a hammer which lay near, raised it in her hands as if she would strike the model of the child, and destroy it.

"Hilda!" cried Max, seizing her wrists and struggling with her.

"It shall not part us!" she cried passionately.

"Hush! here is Lisbeth," whispered Max.

"Is it not lovely?" said Lisbeth, coming in on tip-toe, and speaking softly as if in a sacred place. "See, dear Max, how Hilda loves my children. One of them sleeps alive in her arms"—pointing to the bed—"another sleeps here in death always before our eyes, by the magic of her hands. Ah, what a tender mother our clever Hilda will be!"

Hilda burst into tears, dropped the hammer, and turning abruptly to the window, leaned her arms on the sash, and wept with sobs into the night.

"She has never quite got over the death of that child," murmured Lisbeth. "Come away, Max, and let her have her cry in peace."

An hour later still, Lisbeth was sitting spinning at her door in the moonlight, and singing to herself simple songs about little child-angels who sometimes come down for a time, and live in good men's houses, and lie in fond mother's arms, but after a time have to go back to heaven.

At a little distance Max and Hilda were walking up and down, their faces now gleaming in the shade under the trees, their figures now casting shadows in the light of the moon. Round them lay a great circling abyss of gloomy darkness, fringed with black pine-tops and crowned by frowning crags; and a silver veil was hanging over all.

"What I mean is this," Hilda was saying; "you forget that I am a woman, and judge me by yourself. You think that because you have taught me to model in clay a little, that I must want to be an artist and conquer the world. But you are my world, and I will conquer no other!"

Max's clasp tightened on her hand.

"You must not deny your own power."

"But I am jealous of it, and I hate it. Whenever it comes before you as today, as tonight, a cloud covers your face, and a shadow rises up between us. Though you love the woman, you would banish the artist from your heart; and therefore, Max, because I love you, I will kill that power that disturbs you in me. Never while I live will I touch clay again."

"Then you will make me a murderer, a destroyer of one of Heaven's best gifts."

"Rather I will save you from being the murderer of my heart. Why, oh! why will you not let me be happy? I would rather bake your bread and sweep your floor than be owner of the best studio in Rome."

"Would we were there side by side, Hilda. Without you my inspiration will be gone; my works will be dull and dead."

"Because your coffee will not be as good as some I could make for you."

"Because I shall be without your suggestions, your criticism, your touch that calls life into a face. What would I not give to possess that magic touch!"

"Me, perhaps," said Hilda sadly. "I would die to give it to you—that is, if it has any existence."

Max shuddered.

"Do not talk of dying," he said. "If you were to die there is no kind of death so hateful as my life would become."

"Hush!" said Hilda, putting her fingers across his lips; "only the good God knows anything about death."

Summer deepened, and as the time approached for Max's departure for Rome he found it more and more difficult to think of tearing himself away from Hilda.

"You are my inspiration, my soul," he said. "Without you I shall fail, and be only half a sculptor."

"Dear Max, I will come to you whenever you can send for me. Do you think the mountains will not be dreary, and the very children's voices sad in my ears till I can stand by your side again?"

"Hilda, would you dare—would you venture to come with me?"

"With you?" Hilda's pale face coloured to the hue of a rose for a moment, and turned paler than before. She trembled and drew her breath hard; and then she spoke with the gladness of a bird's song in her voice: "If you will dare it, Max, why so will I."

All the shadows disappeared at once from the young man's face, and his eyes shone.

"You may have hardships to endure, my darling," he said, kissing her hands rapturously.

"They will be welcome," laughed Hilda, "if only to prove how strong I am. You mean to walk across the mountains, Max, and so will I, if you will take me. What an autumn walk it will be! And once in Rome, why, Max, I will save your money by my economy."

"*Your* money, Hilda!"

"Ah, Max, you forget that the cast of your nymph has gone on before us, and that before we get there she may be sold."

"Heaven grant it!" cried Max, while a lightning flash crossed his face. "If I were ambitious before, my Hilda, I am ten times more ambitious now."

Hilda was one of those women to whom no personal sacrifice is too great to add, be it ever so little, to the happiness of the beloved. She was well aware that in accompanying Max hardships and difficulties were awaiting her, but she also knew that with her by his side Max would have better courage to cope with and conquer the world. She said to herself that she would eat little, labour hard, patch and mend her clothes and his, do all that lay within her to cover the extra expense of her presence in his home.

They were married in a little church in their mountains, with a band of children smiling round them, and Lisbeth weeping behind their backs. Oh, why had not Max been satisfied to remain a carver of wood at home? Then Hilda need not have left her kindred, and might have flourished among them through long and happy days. Why, indeed, good Lisbeth? Yours is one of those questions which can never be answered.

The day after their marriage they set out to cross the mountains on foot. A wallet on Max's shoulder held all their luggage, a purse sewn into Hilda's dress contained their wealth. Glorious autumn weather reigned over the mountain world. The hollows under the pines had never looked so purple, the peaks and crags so roseate, the clouds so gold, the firmament so blue as when Max, the sculptor, with his wife by the hand, went trudging along the narrow paths that led the way from Innsbruck up to Trent.

In this memorable journey they spent their honeymoon. In the morning travelling bravely over the rough roads, climbing rude heights, the while hardly daring to expend their breath in speech; at noon cooling their tired feet in some running water, and eating their frugal dinner under the deep broad shadow of the pines. At evening saying a prayer at some simple shrine, and afterwards stepping on gaily through the cooler atmosphere, seeing the sunset colours fade along the mountains, and the moonshine come forth to light them upon yet another mile of the way. Nights spent in the rudest châlets, a day stolen here and there to explore some town through which they passed; endless happy conversations about their love, their art, their future, the heaven of united life that lay on before them; so was accomplished the passage of the mountains, not the greatest of the difficulties that lay in their path, by Edelstein and Hilda his wife.

Through the queer old streets of Verona they walked, and under its lofty arches; and then away across the Italian plains, dropping like a pair of swallows into art-galleries and churches, but hurrying ever with eager steps towards Rome. And there they stood at last one day, weary, dusty, poor, and friendless, but glad at heart and full of hope.

A studio and two rooms were hired at once, and Max went to work upon marble and clay.

The nymph was not sold, but what of that? It would do to furnish the studio till other works were created by the sculptor's hand. Hilda's ingenuity was exerted to make the vast, almost empty rooms which were their dwelling look homelike and gay. A curtain here, a spray of flowers there, a rude vase of fine form and striking colour in a corner; trifles like these made a home out of a wilderness. Singing, sewing, tripping in and out on household errands, or standing behind her husband's shoulder discussing his work with him, Hilda's days were as happy as a queen's. They were in Rome, they were together; Max had lost his melancholy, and he had forgotten his strange fancy about that genius of hers which surely never could have existed. If he remembered it at all he but glanced at it pleasantly, and the thought of it passed easily away. If in moments of depression he called her to him and asked her to touch his work, she would answer reproachfully that her hands were full of flour, and that his dinner must spoil were she to soil them with his clay!

Winter and spring passed over, the little store of money had diminished sadly, and no work of Max's had been sold to replenish the household purse. Hilda held the said purse, and always spoke cheerfully of its contents to Max, who, rapt in his dreams, scarcely realised how the passing days were running away with silver and gold. Neither did he notice that Hilda's always pale face was growing paler and paler. Accustomed to gazing on faces of marble, he was not so struck with her pallor as another might have been, and the look of care always disappeared from her eyes when his were turned upon her. Max in Rome, conscious of growing power, with a brain full of beautiful things as yet uncreated, had all he wanted, and noticed nothing wrong. His home was bright and pleasant, and the food he needed was regularly placed before him. The long summer in Rome did not tell upon his strength as it told upon hers, but, as she did not complain, he was not aware that she had become less healthy than of old.

It was when winter came round again that Hilda took fear to her heart in earnest, and counted the money that was left with paling lips. How could she tell Max that the funds were so low? She would not tell him. And yet, where could she find money to go on with?

Then it was that she broke her resolution never to touch clay again.

On the chill winter mornings when Max was sleeping soundly, having got to rest late at night, Hilda would creep into the studio and go to work. What she produced there Max little dreamed of; but from time to time sundry small, graceful, and original figures found their way into shops where such things are sold. They were quickly disposed of, and the money they fetched replenished Hilda's exhausted purse. She jealously guarded her secret, and Max toiled on, dreaming of glorious works he was to do in the future, and only occasionally waking up to observe that Hilda was a wonderful manager of their slender means.

He never guessed that she was giving her health, her talents, her life for the pittance that supported them both from one week on to another.

It was by means of these little figures of Hilda's that the nymph came to be sold after all. She was in the habit of going in, on her way to market in the mornings, to speak to the dealer who had her works in charge, and to learn if any orders had been left for her.

One day an English gentleman was standing in conversation with the dealer when she appeared, and as she entered the shop she heard the words:

"Here, sir, is the lady herself!"

The gentleman was young and of fair complexion, and had a shrewd, sensible, and withal refined and sympathetic face. He bowed to Hilda, and made known his business at once. He wanted two other original figures besides those of hers he had already bought.

Hilda took the order; and then, with a sudden impulse, said:

"If you would kindly come to see me at my home, my husband could show you something more worthy of your attention."

The stranger was interested, and promised to call as she desired. Then she said with a little embarrassment:

"Please do not speak to my husband of these figures of mine. I do not wish him to know of their existence. He would think I fatigued myself."

The stranger took in the situation at once, bowed, and assured her he would remember her wishes. He thought she looked thoroughly fatigued, indeed, and wondered for a moment how long she would have the power so to exhaust herself. And this was the beginning of the friendship between Max Edelstein and Donald Stewart, which lasted through so many years after.

That very day Donald paid his first visit to the studio, and bought the nymph with Hilda's features, paying for it with a noble sum.

The patronage of the wealthy Englishman, or rather Scotsman, was all that was needed to bring Edelstein's genius into notice. Money and orders for work flowed upon him, and the crisis of his fortune was past.

Many new comforts appeared in his home, and Hilda no longer rose in the chill hours to do secret work with her hands in the clay. Her figures were seen no more in the shops, her artistic efforts were all in the past, and on the sweet spring days she lay on a couch at her window, with her eyes fixed steadfastly on the everlasting hills.

Still Max did not see that she was dying. Donald Stewart did, and to him she spoke of her approaching death.

"Do not disturb Max," she said to this good friend, when he would come from the studio into her little sitting-room to visit her. "He thinks I shall be strong soon, and his thoughts are with his work. One day, I know, he will astonish the world, and in that day he will not so much need me. Nay, I do not mean to doubt his heart. I know he loves me well, and, perhaps, will never love another. But he has passed the point up to which he needed a woman's devoted love and care."

"When does a man cease to need that?" said Donald Stewart.

Hilda was gazing wistfully at the purple hills.

"During the next twenty years," she said, "Max will live in his art alone. His own creations will be his idols, sweetened to him by my memory, which will cling around them. His life will pass in the happy throes of work such as his, and he will hardly miss me from his home. After twenty years have passed—"

She paused, and a look of intense pity and longing settled in her eyes.

"Who can look so far ahead as twenty years?" said Stewart, guessing her thought.

"At the end of that time he will begin to need me again," said Hilda. "The first harvest of life will be won, the desire for a little rest will have begun to awake in him. He will look around and want me at his fireside. Oh, God! that I then could come back to him!"

Stewart's eyes filled with tears.

"A strange idea!" he said softly. "But I have no doubt or fear but that you will really be near him. Your spirit will never lose sight of him."

Hilda smiled.

"Never!" she said. "Never, as God is good! But oh, I meant more than that. If the Creator would but grant me my heaven in letting me return, even years hence, to this world to Max!"

Donald's heart was shaken by the pathetic cry in her voice; but he knew not what to answer to so startling a speech.

"Do not be shocked at me, Mr. Stewart," she said, turning to him with one of her old smiles; "but this is an idea that at times charms away my pain. And if I come," she added playfully, laying her little palms together like a child at prayer, "I will come without the talent which I believe was the only flaw that Max could ever see in me. Anything of genius I may have I hereby solemnly bequeath to my husband. If I come again from heaven, I come without it."

In the flush of the Roman spring she slipped away from them almost unawares one morning; and covered with Italian wild flowers she was laid in her grave.

Max took her death in a way that surprised even Donald Stewart. He appeared stunned, and unable to realise what had happened. So happy had he been in their late good fortune that this sudden and unforeseen ending of all their joy seemed to unhinge his mind. He became dull, absent, almost stupid, absorbed in the memory of Hilda, whose presence was still around him, and whom he could not let go into the past. He did not hear when spoken to, took no part in the life around him, neglected his work, and forgot to enter his studio. Orders remained unfinished, and people began to say that the promising young sculptor had got softening of the brain. He would not stir from Rome that summer, nor leave the rooms where Hilda's dresses and little ornaments and possessions still held their place as if they might be needed at any moment. Through all the dangers of that hot season in Rome Donald stuck fast by his side; and when at last Max fell ill of a terrible fever, Donald took the place of a nurse by his bed.

Thanks to his friend's unwearied efforts, Max arose out of this sickness, but pale and cadaverous like the living skeleton of himself. His mind seemed clearer now, and, on the first occasion when, sitting in Hilda's chair at the window, he spoke to Stewart of his wife, he wept like a child over his vanished happiness. He blamed himself bitterly for his conduct to her in many ways. Having learned from the dealer who had sold her wonderful little figures how hard she had worked to produce and dispose of them unknown to him, he made a misery of this proof of her unselfish devotion to him.

"I knew she had distinct genius," he said, "and if I had insisted on her developing it she might have been alive today.

She denied herself sleep, and suffered cold and weariness to provide the money which I was stupid enough not to perceive she must have earned."

"Her love was indeed limitless," said Stewart consolingly, "but you need not blame yourself. She had no wish to develop a separate genius from yours. She said to me—"

"What?" said Edelstein. "Anything that she said I must hear."

"That if she could come back to you, she would come without that talent which she thought you magnified, and which she did not love in herself."

"Come back?"

"Yes; it was an odd thing to say, but another proof of her devotion to you. It grew out of a conversation I had with her one day."

"When I was wrapped up in my selfish work. When you saw what was coming and I would not."

"That was her comfort. She dreaded a lingering trial for you."

"If she could come back! Did she say that, Donald?"

"She said—I think there is no harm in my repeating to you her tender and fantastic thought—she said she could wish that God would give her heaven by allowing her to come back to you twenty years hence."

"Twenty years hence?"

"She thought for twenty years you could live absorbed in the splendid labours that are around and before you. After that—"

"Ay?"

"After that you would want her more. I understood her to mean that if she could return to you then, as young and sweet as she was a year ago, then, when your genius had slaked its thirst for work, and, a little tired, you might look round for companionship and human love, that so to come would be the desire of her soul."

A strange light came on Edelstein's face, brightening steadily into a glow of exultation.

"Do you think she will come, Donald?"

Stewart started and stared. He felt a qualm of fear that he had been unwise in speaking as he had done, while his friend's brain might be still in a delicate state.

"I think, dear old fellow," he said gently, "that such a fancy of hers only assures you that she will watch and wait for you in eternity. Who can count on living twenty years? And two like you will be sure to clasp hands when you at last have passed the verge of the grave."

"But that was not what she meant," said Max almost querulously. "Since I have survived her death I may live to be a hundred. And she spoke of twenty years. Mark me, Donald, she will come! I must get on with my work, and be ready to receive her."

Stewart was pained and puzzled by the strange manner in which Max fastened on this fanciful idea. He said no more then, but could not fail to notice how this conversation formed a sort of turning-point in his friend's convalescence. Max began to recover in earnest, and now worried himself because his weakness prevented his returning to work at once. A little more alarmed for his friend's mind than for his bodily health, Stewart determined to leave no effort unmade to restore the poor fellow to his normal state of health and strength; and, being himself a rich man, he saw his way to providing the necessary care and change for the invalid who interested him so much. He ordered his yacht to come to meet them in the Mediterranean; and packing up Max he carried him away for a summer's cruise across the world.

The voyage was a great success, and Edelstein was, or appeared to be, completely restored to health of body and mind. He no longer talked despondingly, and ceased altogether to speak of his dead wife. Donald was almost inclined to blame him for this, and said to himself that, after all, those who sorrow most wildly for bereavement are apt to be those who forget the soonest. Edelstein did not return to Rome, but set up a studio in Paris. After that the star of his fortunes rose higher and higher. Stewart had married and settled down on his Scottish estate, and only occasionally saw or heard of his friend during a few days spent from time to time in the French capital, or by a short but affectionate letter penned in moments of weariness by the great sculptor to his friend. And so the years went over; and the name of Max Edelstein was of European fame.

Twenty years passed away. Edelstein had been established long in London, and many of his most beautiful works had been created for, and prized by Englishmen. Unbounded success was his, and admiration and adulation had been poured out upon him. Nevertheless, he lived in his work alone, had few friends, took long walks with his pipe for sole companion, and was never to be seen in large social gatherings. His only society was that of one or two friends who sometimes dined with him in his perfectly appointed house. In women he felt no interest whatever, and would not have their company, no matter how flatteringly it might be offered to him. Invitations from great ladies dropped into his hands, but they failed to bring him captive into even the most charming drawing-rooms. People said it was affectation, moroseness, conceit which made him live the life of a recluse in the heyday of his fame. But Edelstein did not hear, or did not heed what they had to say.

II.

On a certain hot night in the end of June, Max Edelstein sat at his lonely dinner-table with wine before him which he did not drink. His eyes were fixed on the opposite wall with a strange look of intense expectation mingled with longing. From time to time a slight frown of impatience contracted his brows, his fingers moved restlessly, lifted the glass of wine, but set it down again untasted; and then again the nerves of his face relaxed, and, as if obedient to a familiar self-control, the whole man dropped back into a quiescent state of thought.

Twenty years had made a great change in the youthful sculptor of Innsbruck. His dark locks had changed to silver-white, but, waving and plentiful as they were, this peculiarity only enhanced the beauty of a singularly vigorous and noble countenance. His dark eyes burned under a brow on which intellectual power sat enthroned. The dreamy sadness which lurked in some of the lines of the face had no weakening effect on its general expression, but just tempered the overwhelming force that was visible in every feature and every movement of the head. After sitting for an hour wrapped in his reverie he got up, and leaving the room, walked down a long passage to his studio, which was at the back of the house.

Here a lamp burned low, and he did not turn the flame to a fuller height, but paced up and down the large room, till by degrees the white figures around him became quite visible to his eyes in the semi-darkness. With folded arms and head sunk on his breast, he continued thus to give himself up to his thoughts or dreams, and at last paused before a statue at the feet of which burned the lamp which gave its dim light to the place. It was the marble statue of the nymph which bore Hilda's features, and which had been touched to greater tenderness of expression by her fingers in the days of their betrothal and in the spring of their lives. This first work of his, sold to Donald Stewart, had been returned to him by that faithful friend after Hilda's death, and for it he had substituted a work of equal beauty which held a high place of honour in the Scotsman's home.

As Edelstein stood gazing at the features, dimly seen, but kissed to warmth by the red light of the lamp, a knock came on the door, and before the owner of the studio had time to express impatience at being interrupted, the door opened, and somebody came in.

"Max!"

Edelstein uttered a kind of cry, strange to hear from the lips of such a man.

"You, Donald?" he said, after a moment's struggle with some violent emotion. "I thought—it was someone else."

"Are you not going to welcome me, old fellow?" said Stewart, struck by something strange in his friend. "And why are you mooning here alone in the dark?"

"We artists have ways of our own of going on," said Edelstein, with a short laugh. "But you are welcome, indeed, my friend." And he seized Donald's hand in both his own, and almost crushed it with the energy of his grip. "When were you not welcome?"

"All right, old fellow! Get some more light, that I may see how you are thriving."

Edelstein struck a match, and applied it to a large lamp on a bracket.

"I never let servants in here if I can help it," he said; offered a box of cigars to his friend, lit his own pipe, and the two smoked for a few minutes in silence.

Stewart watched his friend's face as it settled back into its habitual lines, and something that he saw there and did not like, something indescribable which he had seen there before on occasions, but never so plainly as now, disturbed him.

He scarcely knew how to begin a conversation, so full was his mind of something he did not venture to mention; but Max saved him the trouble of starting a subject.

"Donald," he said suddenly, "do you remember what night this is?"

"Ah!" said Stewart.

"This night twenty years ago I held Hilda dead in my arms."

"My dear friend—" began Stewart.

"And some months later you told me of something she said."

"Said?"

"About coming back."

"Max!"

"Stewart, I am expecting her. That is why I started when you came in at the door. I thought it was she."

"Good Heaven, Edelstein! Are you in earnest?"

"Earnest?" said Edelstein, laying down his pipe. "Am I a man to jest, and on such a subject?"

"Are those we love allowed to come back?" Stewart said gently, trying to control his uneasiness and to speak naturally.

"Of that I know nothing. She never broke a promise, and her love was perfect. That is all I know."

"I do not believe in ghosts," said Stewart gravely.

"Ghosts! Nor I; she will not come as a ghost, Donald. She will come as my wife, real as herself, to live with me and comfort me for the rest of my life."

Stewart was silent. The words fell heavily on his heart. Max had overworked himself, and his friend remembered painfully how, many long years ago, certain fears for his friend had troubled his mind.

"Max, old fellow," he said, "if Providence should alter the usual order of Nature's laws to comfort a heart so noble as yours, I, for one, will rejoice, as I think you know. In the meantime, come out of this place for a while. You work too hard, and live too much alone."

"Where shall I go?"

"Take my advice for once, and let me take you, not for a solitary ramble, but into a crowd. Believe me, old friend, you have been doing yourself harm. Strange ideas are getting into your brain. There can be nothing like a complete change for putting you straight."

Max passed his hand over his head.

"I believe you are right, Stewart. I want a change. I will do anything you bid me."

"First of all then, before we make further plans, come off with me now to Lady B——'s. I am intimate with her, and she will only be too proud to receive you."

Edelstein winced.

"I cannot bear a ball-room," he said. "The sight of dancing has a curious effect upon me. I think of whirling dervishes. Now our dancing in the mountains—" He stopped, as a vision, clear and vivid as if only seen yesterday, arose before his eye, of Hilda and himself dancing among the children and neighbours, in the light of the sinking sun, under the shadow of the purple hills.

"There will be no dancing. It is only a solemn reception. There will be a brilliant crowd, and we will just walk through. You need not speak unless you like, and we will come away any moment you please."

"It is sorely against the grain," said Max; "but I will go to please you." He rose, and made a weary movement of hand to head. "You will wait a few minutes while I dress. Stewart," he added, suddenly turning his hand on the door, and making a step towards his friend, "forgive me if I seem ungracious. I am going not only to please you, but to escape from myself. These rooms have begun to seem haunted to me. Something has been going wrong. I will shake off a weakness."

"All right," said Stewart. "Blues from over-work, and over-concentration of thought in one spot. I know all about it, though I am not a worker."

Half an hour afterwards they entered a brilliantly lighted house in St. James's, and were soon moving through a crowd composed of many of the most distinguished men and women in London. The hostess, who had seen Edelstein's noble face before, in his own studio, was gratified at his appearance in her rooms, and received him with flattering kindness. At a whispered word from Stewart, however, she allowed him to pass on into the crowd where few knew him by sight, owing to the extremely retired life which he had hitherto led.

"He is not very well," Donald said to Lady B——, "and I have coaxed him out for once. But we must not frighten him. If a fuss is made about him he will go back into his shell."

And tact being one of Lady B——'s virtues, she took no further notice of the famous sculptor.

Out of one magnificent room into another the friends sauntered, keeping together, till at last Stewart paused to talk to some friends who greeted him warmly and held him fast, and Edelstein, straying on alone, found his way into a drawing-room smaller than the others, with walls panelled in faint gold-coloured silk, upon which a few rare deep-toned pictures were shown to the fullest advantage. There he took up his position at a corner of the tall carven mantelpiece, and looked abstractedly round the place, with the air and with the feeling of a man who has no part in the lives of the people by whom he finds himself surrounded. Suddenly his eyes became fixed, and an extraordinary change passed over his countenance.

A shifting of the groups of people who occupied the centre of the room took place, and an opening in the crowd showed him the figure of a woman dressed in white, sitting against the corner of an antique cabinet, and looking like a picture of St. Barbara with her tower rising straight behind her. She was a girl about twenty, exceedingly fair and pale, with a quantity of that faint-gold hair which belongs to babes, and which near the delicate yellow in the silken panels looked strangely approaching to silver. Although womanly in figure there was a certain snowily ethereal look about her, the only deep touch of colour lying in the depths of her blue and crystal-clear eyes. She had a lonely look, and the air of awaiting someone whom she expected to come for her, and she seemed as little belonging to the crowd as Edelstein himself. She was gazing through the doorway near, yet as if seeing nothing, utter unconsciousness of self in her face and attitude.

It is said that if one human being looks long and intently at another, the person so observed will soon feel the effect of the unseen gaze, and be constrained to meet it. However that may be, the fair-haired girl turned her graceful head after some time, and looked straight across the room at Edelstein, who was gazing at her with Heaven knows what expression of recognition and rapture in his eyes. A shock of surprise passed over her, and then a puzzled look crossed her face, as if she thought she ought to know the distinguished-looking person who thus seemed to claim her acquaintance, and was embarrassed at not remembering his identity.

At this moment Stewart reached the room and stood by his friend's side, who did not see him, but started at hearing the Scotsman's voice at his ear.

"Look, Donald, there she is," said Edelstein, in a low voice thrilling with emotion, and without removing his eager gaze from the white-clad girl at the other side of the room.

"She! Who?" asked Donald, startled by his tone and manner.

"Hilda—my wife," murmured Max, in a voice in which, low as was the utterance, an agony of joy and amazement spoke.

"Max, are you aware of how oddly you are looking at that lady, who is a perfect stranger to you?" said Stewart, and passed his hand through his friend's arm, trying to draw him away.

"Stranger!" said Edelstein, with a little laugh of joy. "Do you mean to say, man, that you do not recognise her?"

"I do indeed see a curious likeness, Edelstein, but surely I need hardly say to you, be yourself, and do not give way to hallucination."

Max did not appear to hear him.

"See how she looks at me!" he muttered, as the girl once more turned her fascinated eyes, half frightened, half attracted, on his. "Donald, do not hold me back. I must go and claim her. Oh, Heaven! how strange to meet in such a place as this!"

Stewart was shocked and agitated at this unexpected result of his attempt to cure his friend of a monomania. Amazed himself at the extraordinary resemblance in the girl before him to the long-lost Hilda, who slept in her Italian grave, he could only think of one way of cutting short so painful a moment as this, and strove to induce Edelstein to quit the room with him.

But another glance at Max told him he must humour the great sculptor as he would humour a madman.

"Listen to me, Edelstein," he said. "Even if it be she, there are certain rules of etiquette to be observed. We must ask our hostess to introduce you to her."

"What, to my own wife?"

"Yes. No one here knows that she is your wife, except yourself, and you would not appear to be rude to a lady?"

"You are right, Donald—always right."

"Come then, and let us lose no time."

Stewart had hoped to make his friend forget this craze, and tried to lead him into other rooms, to interest him in the sculptures of an old and richly decorated mansion; but he found that such a hope was vain, for Edelstein dragged him straight to Lady B——'s presence, and obliged him to ask for the desired introduction.

"Lady B——, my friend Mr. Edelstein wishes to be introduced to a certain young lady in white in the yellow drawing-room. Can you kindly gratify his wish?"

"I can guess who she is," said Lady B——, pleased at the interest shown by the great artist, usually so indifferent, in a favourite of her own. "She is Miss Trevelyan, a peculiarly beautiful and striking girl."

Max smiled a strange smile at Stewart, as if to say: "We will humour this amiable woman, and keep our own secret for the present," and then both men followed their hostess as she moved towards the yellow drawing-room.

The introduction was made, Lady B—— returned to the friends who required her presence elsewhere, and Edelstein stood by the girl in white, trying to frame a sentence with his trembling lips.

Stewart also stood by, having been introduced to the lady, and endeavoured, by his matter-of-fact remarks, to restore equanimity to two evidently embarrassed people. An acquaintance coming up claimed his attention for a few minutes; he was obliged to stand aside to let some ladies pass; in the crowd he drifted to some distance. When he was once more disengaged, he turned to look for his friend, but Edelstein and the lady were gone.

With a misgiving which he could not smother, Donald Stewart set out to search the rooms for his friend. After an interval of half an hour, and when he was almost thinking of returning to Edelstein's house, to seek him there, he at last discovered the sculptor and the white lady sitting in a retired nook half behind a curtain, and at an open window, beyond which the lighted tower of Westminster was seen to loom and burn in the purple-dark midnight sky.

The sculptor's fine head was in relief against the sky, and he was gazing in his companion's face with an intensity of love and joy which no words could express. What he was saying Donald could not hear, but he was pouring forth rapid words in a low impassioned voice. The girl was pale as death, and sat listening like a person who strives to remember, her eyes fixed on Edelstein's face. A look of awe was on her broad white brow, and with a strange, almost supernatural feeling which he could not account for, Stewart felt shocked at her amazing likeness to the long dead and buried Hilda.

"Edelstein," said Stewart, "excuse me, but I think you said you were anxious to leave this place early, and it is now about half-past twelve."

Max looked up at him with a smile. Without noticing his words, he turned to the lady, and taking her hand, laid it in Stewart's, saying:

"Hilda, this is our dear good friend Donald. You remember Donald, my Hilda?"

The girl suffered her hand to rest in Stewart's, and murmured dreamily:

"Yes, I remember; he seems quite familiar to me."

"Good Heavens!" thought Stewart, "has my madman met with a madwoman to complete his ruin? or has she found out that he is mad, and is she humouring his whim through fear?"

"Miss Trevelyan," he said, relinquishing her hand, "I must beg you to excuse the peculiarity of my friend's conduct in addressing you so, and by a name that is not yours. He has not been well, and I see that he is hardly himself."

"They call me Hilda," said the girl, looking strangely and reproachfully at Stewart. "Why should he address me by another name?"

Then she turned her face again towards Max, who seemed at once to forget Donald's presence; and they continued their low-voiced communing as though he had not been there.

Amazed and pained Stewart turned away, and uncertain how to act, found himself in the room with Lady B——, his hostess.

"Lady B——," he said, "my friend Edelstein is greatly taken with your friend, Miss Trevelyan. By the way, what is her Christian name?"

"Hilda. Why do you ask?"

"I have a fancy in ladies' names."

" 'Tis a pretty name, and, by the way, a story is told of a curious dream her mother had which was the cause of her being so called. They are Cornish people, and the girl is full of romance. So was the mother, who is dead."

"You interest me greatly," said Donald. "My friend seems wonderfully taken with her."

"Don't let him put his heart into the matter," said Lady B——, laughing, "for the child is already engaged. It is a long story, and she has been very troublesome. Were I to tell you the whole you would understand why I call her romantic."

Lady B—— turned away to answer a question asked from another side, and Stewart stood musing perplexedly over the information he had received.

"Already engaged! And Max calls her his wife!" he reflected. "The girl is full of romance; and to me she seemed quite ready to obey his thought. There is a storm of trouble in the air, if I cannot get Max out of England by tomorrow night. And yet he may forget all this tomorrow morning, if he be the madman I fear I must take him to be."

After some time spent very uneasily, Stewart went back to the window where he had left his friend with the lady he had called his wife. Both were gone.

Five minutes afterwards he met Edelstein coming through the crowd to meet him with a beaming countenance.

"They took her away," he said, with a slight laugh, "the people who are her friends. I could not object, of course, and we are parted for the present. But think of it, Stewart, letting my own wife go away with strangers! But I shall see her tomorrow, and explain everything to her father."

Donald felt sick at heart. He was too much perplexed and troubled to try to reason with his friend, and besides, he feared to quarrel with a madman. He accompanied Edelstein home, and went with him into his studio.

As they stood before the statue whose face had been modelled from Hilda's, Max raised the lamp till the red light fell full on the marble features.

"Look, Donald, look! she has not changed one atom!"

The likeness was indeed marvellous. Even Stewart acknowledged that the two Hildas were, outwardly at least, the same.

"My dear fellow," he said, "I acknowledge that there is a startling resemblance; but go to sleep on this, and tomorrow your thoughts will be more clear. You must not make people talk about Miss Trevelyan."

Max smiled a peculiar smile.

"You think I am mad, Stewart," he said; "I know you think I am mad. But can she be mad too? That would be too singular a coincidence."

"Do you mean to tell me that the young lady you met for the first time tonight has declared that she knows herself to be your dead wife, returned to this world to be with you?"

"You have put it into excellent words, good Donald. Knowing your sceptical mind, I almost shrank from stating the facts to you so plainly."

"My poor Max!"

"Tush, Donald! don't put me in a passion. Did you yourself not solemnly convey to me her promise?"

"She made no promise, Max. It was the fond and futile wish of a dying woman that I unfortunately repeated to you. Your wife was too sensible, too religious a woman to believe that such return from the dead could ever be."

"There is nothing in religion to forbid such belief," said Max doggedly. "She has returned out of her heaven by the force of her all-powerful love. She was re-born into this world the very year after she quitted it."

"I wish you would go to bed, Edelstein, and sleep upon it."

Max smiled.

"After twenty years of silence I have talked with my wife tonight," said he, "and I have much to think over before I can sleep. But, dear old friend, I would not keep you here wrangling with me. When I have recovered a little from the shock of this wonderful happiness I shall be able to thank you for being the bearer, a second time, of a blessing into my life. Meantime take your rest. When you have got over your natural surprise you will wake up and recognise my Hilda."

Donald left his friend, feeling half-stunned with amazement at the occurrences of the night. That Max, whom he believed to be mad, should reason with him pityingly, as if his were the weaker mind, seemed to finish the extreme oddity of the whole situation. His only hope for Edelstein lay now in the likelihood that the girl might lead the way out of the confusion of this hour. If indeed she had been subject to some spell while in Edelstein's presence, perhaps when no longer under his personal influence she might be roused to see the folly of the position in which she placed him as well as herself. Before laying his head on his pillow that night Stewart resolved to go in the morning, as early as might be, and to ask an interview with the woman whom Edelstein claimed as his wife.

The next morning, however, Donald remembered that he must go to Lady B—— for Miss Trevelyan's address, and on his way to that lady he decided on opening his mind to her at once as Miss Trevelyan's friend; at least in as far as he dared. He was fortunate in finding Lady B—— at home.

"I have come to you on a curious errand," he said; "I want you to give me some account of Miss Trevelyan's character, disposition, and circumstances. I am prompted by no idle curiosity."

"You come in the interest of your friend the sculptor," said the lady, "who evidently fell in love with her last night. If her father had been here he would hardly have been pleased, for I think I mentioned to you he has already promised her to another man."

"He has promised her?"

"Well that is the way to put it. The girl is, as I told you, full of romance. She has been brought up in a gloomy old house on a wild Cornish coast, without a mother and without youthful friends and companions. She is dreamy and sentimental, and has fancies about herself."

"Every woman has a right to a little of that kind of thing," said Stewart, who had married his own wife for love. "Heaven knows there are enough women of a different type. I suppose the man her father has chosen is rich?"

"Enormously wealthy, and very much in love with her. 'Tis true he is neither young nor interesting. He is a City banker; and Mr. Trevelyan is a needy, almost a ruined man."

"You mean that there is not a glimpse of hope for my friend Edelstein?"

"I think there is none."

"But if she herself should prefer him? He is not poor, and he is a distinguished man. And he is probably younger than the person of her father's choice."

"Considerably so, I should say, and a thousand times more fascinating, I am sure. In every way more desirable, I believe. Nevertheless, his suit is hopeless."

"Lady B———, I will confide in you wholly. My friend is no common man. Early in life he married a wife whom he tenderly loved, and whose untimely death almost unhinged his brain. Miss Trevelyan bears an extraordinary resemblance to the dead Hilda."

"Hilda! How odd!"

"Yes; the case is full of peculiarities. Now I greatly fear that if Edelstein should continue to see Miss Trevelyan, and afterwards lose her, the total wreck of his mind may be the consequence. Believe me, I am not over-stating the truth. I appeal to you to ascertain immediately whether there is hope for him or not, and if not, to remove Miss Trevelyan out of his path."

"You make a strange demand, my friend. Why should not Mr. Edelstein be able to take care of himself; or his friends be able to take care of him? Why should the girl's movements be interfered with? She is enjoying her first season in London, and it is only half over. Her father is in Parliament, and it does not suit him to move about just now. How can I ask him to take his daughter out of Mr. Edelstein's way?"

"Dear Lady B———, for the sake of our old friendship I ask you to see what can be done. I myself will do my best to get Max out of London. For the present I will only ask you to see Miss Trevelyan and learn her mind, and appeal to her not to encourage Edelstein."

"There I am all with you. I will see the child at once. Though I cannot but think, friend Donald, that you take an exaggerated view of the situation, and allow your own turn for romance to run away with your judgement."

Late that afternoon Lady B——— took her way to the lodging in St. James's where Mr. Trevelyan and his daughter had taken up their abode for the season. The house and its appointments bore out Lady B———'s assertion that Mr. Trevelyan was a needy if not a ruined gentleman.

She was shown into a rather dingy drawing-room, and in a few minutes the pale girl of the night before, the second

Hilda, came into the room with a radiant countenance. She was dressed in a soft white woollen gown with crimson roses at her throat. Her clear blue eyes were dilated with joy, her face was paler than ever, her fair hair, which shone like mixed gold and silver, glittered softly on her temples, and fell back in a heavy plait on her shoulders. She extended her hands to her friend with a happy, eager movement.

"Why, Hilda, how glorified you look! I am glad to see you looking so happy, my dear."

"Yes, I am happy," said Hilda quietly, and stole her arms round her friend's neck.

"Yet you were rather naughty last night, Hilda, talking so much to that Mr. Edelstein in the absence of your *fiancé*."

The girl withdrew from her friend's embrace, and sat down by her side.

"You do not understand," she said, "and how can I tell you? Mr. Edelstein and I are no new friends."

"Indeed! You surprise me extremely."

"I am sure I do. And I fear I shall also surprise others who love me. But Max has the first and highest claim."

"My dear Hilda, can anything be the matter with my ears?"

"You seem to hear me pretty well."

"Hilda, I am angry with you. You mean to tell me that you have thrown over your betrothed, set your father's will at naught, and all for a stranger?"

"Not for a stranger, Lady B———. I am Max Edelstein's wife."

Lady B——— uttered a cry, and then sat still, gazing at the girl before her.

"You are either quite mad," she said at last, "or you are a double-dealing and unworthy woman."

Hilda smiled mysteriously, and putting her hands on her friend's shoulders kissed her tenderly.

"Do not be angry," she said, "till you hear my story;" and then she sat down at Lady B———'s feet, and began to speak at length, while her friend listened patiently to her tale. The burden of what she had to say was the same as that reiterated by Edelstein to Stewart. She was the Hilda of Innsbruck. She had died, and had promised to return. They had recognised each other on the instant they had met. They were husband and wife, and no strangers of a day. Nobody should dare to part them.

Looking at her innocent, ingenuous face, Lady B——— seized her hands and sighed heavily. Here was a mind gone astray. How sad, how incomprehensible! A lonely unnatural bringing-up had induced eccentricity, a romantic incident had inflamed her imagination, and reason was overturned at a blow. What could be done for this unfortunate girl?

"My friend Stewart knew something of this," she reflected, "and that is why he so urgently desired that they should not meet again. Now, which is the lunatic here? And is lunacy catching, like the measles?"

When Lady B——— reached home again she found Stewart awaiting her return. As she entered her own drawing-room with a scared pale face, Donald came to meet her. She sank into a chair, and Stewart waited impatiently till she was able to speak.

"Your friend is a madman," she said at last.

"That is what I dread," said Stewart sadly. "My only hope for him rested upon the lady. From your manner I conclude that my worst fears are realised."

"What are your worst fears?"

"That she shares his delusion."

"What is his delusion?"

"That his dead wife has fulfilled a promise he fancies she made, and has returned to this world to be near him."

"He has communicated his mania to her."

"What does she say about herself?"

"That she has always been followed by indistinct memories of a former life. That the moment she saw him she recognised him. That everything he told her of the past she instantly recollected. That Heaven has granted them both the boon of her return. That she belongs, and will belong, to no one else but him; and that nothing shall part them but death."

"It seems too strange a coincidence. Yet an imaginative girl might be influenced by a mind like Edelstein's."

"My friend, what shall we do with them?"

"If they could marry they might possibly be happy."

"It can never be, I believe. I, for one, do not like to open the matter to her father. Yet I think he ought to be told."

The next day Lady B—— wrote a carefully worded letter to Mr. Trevelyan, and by night had a short note from him in answer. It said:

"That madman Edelstein has been here, and Hilda and he have told me of their ridiculous story. I have given him my mind; and tomorrow Hilda goes away to friends. Even to you I will not tell where I have sent her. Let her be lost to the world till she has returned to her senses."

The next day Lady B—— handed this note to Mr. Stewart, and Donald at once went off to Edelstein, whom he found lost in grief, having just returned from the Trevelyans' lodgings, where he had learned that the young lady was gone.

Stewart tried to rouse him up.

"Come, come," he said, "be a man and shake this madness off! Think of your wife in heaven, and leave this girl to the disposal of her father. She is already pledged to another man."

"Against her will," said Edelstein calmly. "She herself had given no pledge. How could she, being already my wife? But do not torture me, Donald. She is gone, it is true; but I shall find her again."

"Be it so, old friend. All that I can do to help you I will do. In the meantime, while we are all at fault, come with me to my Scotch mountain-side. There you can get up your strength, and consider what further steps to take."

After much persuasion Edelstein consented to accompany his friend. All his attempts to hear further tidings of Hilda had proved vain, and, as no letter came from her to him, he concluded that she was closely watched. Donald hoped, on the contrary, that she had only returned to her senses.

On a lovely June evening the two friends arrived at the gate leading into Stewart's private grounds in a lovely part of Scotland, and leaving their carriage with the servants, walked up a winding by-path which tacked along a garden-wreathed mountain-side. At their feet lay the sea, guarded by cliffs which were low here and high there, and at one part formed themselves into a sort of lofty bridge leading from Stewart's charming dwelling on the upper heights to the sand-strewn and rock-bound shore beneath.

At one point they stood still to admire the magnificent view, their gaze resting on the violet-tipped peaks in the clouds, and then falling and following the golden light that ran "along the smooth wave towards the golden west;" and Edelstein raised his hat with a gesture of reverent delight.

"Colour is hardly a sculptor's province," he said with a smile; "but I could almost wish at this moment to be a painter."

Donald was delighted.

"I think I can make you happy here," he said, "for a week at least. You can go when you are tired of us."

Edelstein smiled his answer. His thoughts had been carried away to the Alps—to the Roman hills. That delicate violet on these lovely mountains had coloured his imagination with their own suggestions. His soul was away with Hilda on the Alps.

They continued their walk, still climbing, and presently here and there, between bush and scaur, glimpses of Donald's home came into view. One steep path of a few yards remained to be travelled, and at the top of it a figure in white appeared with one arm thrown round a young ash-tree, a figure leaning forward as if watching for their approach. A few more steps, and they were face to face with Hilda.

"Good Heavens!" cried Donald. "Miss Trevelyan – how have you come here?"

She had slipped her hand through Edelstein's arm, and, looking at Stewart frankly, said:

"Ah, Mr. Stewart, what an unkind welcome! How often in the old days have you hoped I should come here!"

Donald turned to his friend.

"What does this mean, Max?" he said. "Has it been a preconcerted plan?"

"If a plan at all, a plan of Providence," said Edelstein, whose face was shining with satisfaction. "The same Power that has sent Hilda back into the world has been able to place her feet upon your hills. That is all I have to say. Hilda will tell us the rest. As for me, I have felt that, turn where I might, I should meet her again."

"My father sent me here," said Hilda. "Indirectly he sent me here. He placed me with his friends a mile away, and Mrs. Stewart met me with them, and invited me to spend a few days with her. I have felt, like Max, that our parting would not be for long. This morning Mrs. Stewart said to me, 'My husband arrives this evening, and he brings with him his old friend, the sculptor, Edelstein.' And I was not the least surprised to hear it."

Then they turned away, hand in hand, just as Hilda and Max used to saunter together on the Alps long ago, and Donald, amazed and troubled, went in at his own door and retired to take counsel with his wife.

Mrs. Stewart was greatly astonished at the tale her husband had to tell.

"I took a fancy to the girl," she said. "There is something so uncommon about her. It was but natural to ask her to come here. The people she was with are stiff and hard in their way, and she seemed so pleased to get away from them."

"It was very natural, Jeanie," said her husband. "And it was also natural in me to bring poor Edelstein here. The coincidence is the part of it that takes away my breath."

"I think we can hardly be to blame," said Mrs. Stewart.

"If Trevelyan had been acquainted with me it could not have happened," said Donald. "But he knows nothing of me and I know little of him. The only thing for me to do now is to write to him stating the case as it stands; and meantime, if possible, to get Edelstein away with me on an excursion somewhere."

The evening passed quietly away. The host and hostess, secretly ill at ease, exerted themselves to appear as if nothing was wrong. At dinner-time Edelstein talked brilliantly, and was so transformed that Donald, his friend of years, scarcely knew him. Hilda appeared in the rich dress of pure white in which he had met her in London, and her face was shining with tranquil happiness. There were no other guests.

As the hours passed by, Mrs. Stewart, who could not detect symptoms of madness in either of her guests, reflected that it was a thousand pities that these two must be parted. Later in the evening Hilda sang Scotch and German ballads—sang the songs that the other Hilda had sung twenty years ago before the door of her Alpine home. Edelstein sat by her side, gazing at her with looks of worship.

After the ladies had retired to rest Stewart put his arm through that of his friend, and drew him out on the terrace overlooking the sea.

"My dear fellow," he said, "fortune has been playing curiously into your hands, I admit; but, you see, I cannot allow this sort of thing to go on. Miss Trevelyan is here by a strange accident. Now, until her father comes or sends to remove her, you must take yourself away. I will go with you on an excursion round the coast—anywhere you like, so that you get out of this house for a time."

Edelstein smiled.

"Donald," he said, "you are the soul of honour, and always were. You would sacrifice even the happiness of your old friend to your idea of honour. I respect you. I feel with you where any other matter than this is concerned. But when you speak of Miss Trevelyan, you forget that you speak of Max Edelstein's wife. That is the one point which I cannot keep before you."

"Man, man!" cried Donald, out of all patience, "will you not give up this unholy craze? Does Providence work miracles for you alone? Come, come, old friend, do not exasperate me!"

"The world is full of miracles, Donald, only we do not perceive them. I will not believe that you do not recognise Hilda."

"I see a startling likeness, but that does not overturn my reason. I see a likeness in person, but many differences in character. The first Hilda had a noble mind, strong clear common sense—nay, she had genius, which is not always allied with the other quality. Miss Trevelyan is weak, imaginative, and without any strength of character."

"I have thought of some differences, and they only strengthen my belief—if, indeed, it needed strengthening. In the first place, you wrong the lady you are pleased to call Miss Trevelyan (and Miss Trevelyan I am willing you should call her till our marriage can be solemnised again). She is not weak in character, as you believe. She is feminine, believing—In short, she knows what you will not admit. As for the genius that once distinguished her—ah, Donald, do you forget what you told me she said when promising to return to me, if she could? 'If I come,' she said, 'I will come without the talent which I believe was the only flaw that Max could ever see in me.' She was wrong there. I saw no flaw in her, and by her talent and devotion she carried me over the worst, the hardest bit of my career; but she thought it. 'Anything of genius I may possess,' she continued, 'I hereby solemnly bequeath to Max.' And herein lies the secret of my later complete success. 'If I come again,' she said, 'I come without it.' "

He drew a little pocket-book out of his breast, and read over again the words in Stewart's writing.

"Do you forget jotting this down," he said, "and afterwards giving it, at my request, to me? I have never parted with it for a moment since you put it in my hands."

"And so have driven yourself mad on one point," said Stewart, aghast at this result of his own well-meant action.

"I am not mad, Donald," said Max quietly, putting the book back in its resting-place; "but these are among the things that are beyond our ken."

"There is no use in battling with a madman," said Stewart to his wife that night. "I cannot bring him to reason, and the girl seems as much astray as he. I have communicated with her father already; in the morning I will write him a fuller account of the unexpected meeting here; and this is all I can do."

"I cannot see that either is mad," said Mrs. Stewart, "and to me it seems like sin to meddle between them. Why can they not marry and be happy in their touching delusion, if delusion it be?"

" 'If delusion it be'!" said Stewart. "My dear, are you losing your senses too?"

"I hope not, Donald. I have always been called matter-of-fact; but I would rather not dwell on this point. I take my stand simply on this—that I would like to see so interesting a pair married and happy."

"There I heartily agree with you; but I am not her father, nor are you her mother; and her father must have his voice in the matter."

Nothing more was said, but early in the morning Stewart rose and went to his study to write his letter to Hilda's father. This written and despatched, he went out to the garden to wait for the summons to breakfast. Returning to the house, he met his wife coming down the path.

"Neither Mr. Edelstein nor Hilda is to be found," she said hurriedly.

"Good Heavens!" said Stewart, "has no one seen them?"

"The gardener saw them about six o'clock this morning."

"Where?"

"Here in the garden. When he arrived to begin his work he met Mr. Edelstein walking about, and looking as if he had not slept all night. Presently Miss Trevelyan appeared, fresh and bright after her sleep, and walked among the roses, gathering them as she went, and splashing herself with dew. She seemed surprised to see Mr. Edelstein. They spoke together for some time, never seeming to notice the presence of the gardener. At last Mr. Edelstein said, 'Come then!' and took her by the hand, and they walked away together hand-in-hand; and then the sun rose high, suddenly, and he could not see where they went for the blaze of light. He thinks they went down towards the cliffs."

"Perhaps they have only gone for a walk," said Stewart, but with a face of anxiety.

Mrs. Stewart shook her head.

"I think," she said, "that you will never see them again till they are indeed man and wife. Hasty marriages are easily made in this country, remember."

"And all your sympathies are with the crazy pair," said Stewart, almost angrily. "You do not think of the trouble that I shall get into with her friends."

Even while the husband and wife talked in the garden, the sky darkened, and great drops of rain began to fall. The wind rose, and there was every sign of a storm.

Stewart, nothing daunted by the weather, set off post-haste in a carriage with a pair of horses to follow in the track of his friend. He felt a conviction that his wife's words were true—that Edelstein had taken the matter into his own hands, and would make Hilda his wife before friends or enemies could interfere.

The route he followed ran along by the sea, and after an hour's driving through the storm he arrived at a small fishing seaport, where he made inquiries among the people. He soon learned that his fears were realised. A lady and gentleman had presented themselves that morning to the clergyman of the place, and had been married. Immediately afterwards they had hired a hooker to carry them, some said to France, some said to Ireland. Half an hour after they left the pier the storm began to rise; many had watched the hooker through a glass with some anxiety, but it had seemed to hold on its way steadily enough, and was now out of sight.

"Ireland or France!" said Mr. Stewart impatiently. "Surely someone knows where they are gone. Who would take them in a hooker from here to France."

"Our hookers will do better work than ye think," said a brawny fisherman. "But I heard them talk about Ireland."

Mr. Stewart was in despair. It did not matter, after all, towards what country the husband and wife had set their faces. He thought bitterly of Lady B—— and her friend, Mr. Trevelyan, and wished impatiently that this extraordinary elopement had taken place from under any roof rather than his own. Of Edelstein's happiness he could not then even think, so vexatious were the circumstances in which he found himself unexpectedly placed.

Stamping up and down the pier while he made his reflections, he scarcely noticed that the storm was becoming wilder every moment, till suddenly a furious gust, almost sweeping him from his foothold, startled him out of his musing, and changed his feeling of anger against the runaway pair into anxious fears for their safety.

Gazing round him after a long look at the now raging sea, he was aware of a group of solemn weather-beaten faces scanning his features with sympathy, and he immediately questioned the men as to the amount of danger to be apprehended from the storm.

"It's a bad day, and it'll be a waur night," said one who made himself spokesman for the rest. "A wad rather yer friens had ta'en their flight by land."

Sick at heart now, Stewart pressed the seafaring men with questions. Their fear was that the hooker would be run upon some of the rocks along the coast. Donald took his way to the inn of the village, where his horses were put up, and decided on sending a message to his wife, and remaining in this place for the night. It did not appear to him that he could effect much good by doing so, yet he felt more within reach of news on this spot than he should have felt in his drawing-room at home.

Towards evening the tempest swelled into a hurricane. One or two houses were flung down in the little town, slates and chimneys from all sides clattered into the street, and the bells from the various points of danger on the rocky coast clanged and tolled the black night through. Stewart walked his room hour after hour, and tried to check his gloomy thoughts by recurring to the suggestion of one of the sailors, that after all the hooker might have put in somewhere along the coast, before the storm became so furious. This was the only hope that presented itself in the midst of horror, and he clung to it with all his might. Nevertheless, as he left his room in the wild scared light of the morning, and went out to look about, he felt a dread at heart that some unforeseen catastrophe had ended the curious drama in which he had been obliged, unwillingly, to take a part.

About twelve o'clock the storm went down, but the weather remained bleak and sullen. Stewart ordered his carriage, and set off by the coast road, stopping at all the dwellings and villages as he went along, asking if a hooker had been harboured or wrecked in the neighbourhood. His search was vain, the answer to questions as to harbour generally was, "No hooker could live in such a hurricane as that of last night."

When it was quite evening, he at last met a man upon the road who had some little news to give him, having heard of people who had been washed in that morning near a village some miles further on by the shore. Yes, there was a man, and there was a woman. The woman was a lady; and had been taken into somebody's house.

Stewart now drove as fast as his horses could carry him, and arrived at the place where the sea had given up its prey. "Oh, ay!" said the folks he met; a sailor-boy and a lady had been washed in alive; a gentleman and one or two others had been drowned. Then a revulsion of feeling swept over Donald Stewart, and his heart cried out for the faithful friend of so many bygone years. If one must be taken, why could it not have been the woman who had lent her weakness to help a great mind to its ruin? He forgot the father who would hold him, Donald Stewart, accountable for the fate of a child; and thought only of his own irreparable loss.

He was taken into a humble fisherman's house, and there, by the fire, sat the sailor-lad who had survived the wreck.

In a few strong words he told the story of the night's catastrophe. The gentleman was as brave as a lion, he said. He lashed the lady to the mast, and that was how she was saved. For himself the gentleman counted surely on his swimming. He was a powerful swimmer, and must have been dashed upon the rocks and stunned. He (the lad saved) could not swim a stroke. These things were well known to be all chance or fate. The waves which had killed the skilful swimmer had but tossed the helpless boy roughly in their embrace, and hurled him safe upon the sand.

In an inner room Hilda was lying upon a bed. She did not speak, but fixed one long, strange look upon Donald Stewart, and then turned away her face to the wall. Stewart sent for his wife immediately, and that kind woman nursed the girl through what proved to be a dangerous illness. When she was sufficiently restored they carried her home to their house, where her father had arrived to meet her.

A rather narrow-minded, unsympathetic man, Mr. Trevelyan was unable to take any lenient view of his daughter's conduct. While she lay in peril of death his grief was extreme, but once she was out of danger his anger rose high again, and he resolved that, as soon as she was able to bear them, his reproaches should be equal to her deserts.

However, when he saw her sit listening to his hard words with an absent, unmoved expression of face, as if she hardly heard him, or did not understand him, his eloquence failed, and he felt more fear than wrath stirring within him.

"What do you think of her?" he asked timorously of Mrs. Stewart.

"I know what you mean," she said, "but I do not find any flaw in her brain; she is simply overwhelmed by a depth of agony which you and I cannot fathom."

"But how can she feel such grief for a man of whom she knew so little? You surely do not believe her story that she lived a former existence and was Edelstein's wife?"

"I cannot tell you exactly what I believe," said Mrs. Stewart with a troubled look. "Perhaps I am a little over-tired myself with anxiety and nursing, but I have been powerfully impressed by the strength and vividness of her own conviction on this subject. Her ravings were most strange. She does not speak about the matter now."

"Try to get her to speak," said the father, who was softening every moment towards his child.

Mrs. Stewart tried to lead her to open her mind on the strange subject which engrossed it. Hilda sat at the window, her fair, almost silvery head set in a framework of roses, her face deadly pale, her eyes darkened with their habitual shadow of grief. Stewart, looking at her, was startled afresh by her extraordinary resemblance to the dying Hilda, who, sitting thus at a window looking out at the Roman hills, had spoken to him those fatal words which he had too faithfully recorded and repeated to her husband. Overwhelmed by an almost supernatural feeling that forced him against his will to share momentarily the delusion of his lamented friend, and to imagine that he saw the Hilda of Rome in the flesh before him, he arose hastily and went out of the room.

"My dear," said Mrs. Stewart, struck by something in the girl's eyes which had suddenly turned on her, "will you not speak to me a little, if only to ease your poor heart?"

"What can I say?" said Hilda, with a wan smile. "There is one thought ever in my mind; and who can share it with me? I rashly asked to have my heaven in returning to the earth to him. My prayer was granted—not for my heaven, but for my purgatory."

"Dear child!"

"And my punishment I shall have to endure. I am not going to die, as you all seem to fear. I shall live many years in my purgatory; and I shall not be allowed to be idle in my pain. Work will be found for me to do."

As soon as she was sufficiently restored to health her father took her away to her old home in Cornwall, where she lived with him as a dutiful and tender daughter till his death, which occurred a few years after these events. But there was always something in her face which seemed to mark her as different from other girls; and no man dared ask her to be his wife.

After her father's death she went abroad, and joined the devoted ranks of the Sisters of Charity. Further we cannot follow her; but she is living still.

The Ghost at Wildwood Chase

It happened only five summers ago. I had had a hard winter and spring of unfitness for work, which, following close on my first successes in Art, had been rather impatiently borne, seeming as they did to destroy my hope while it was budding. Furthermore, I was assured by a doctor that I was threatened with consumption, and I acknowledged that he was probably right, as the disease was in my family. In the beginning of a hot June I sat in my studio in London, weary in body and mind, when a letter came to my hand like a freshening breeze. It was from Lord Wylder, who had bought a picture of mine a few months before, and who now asked me to come down to Wildwood Chase to paint his portrait.

Though not particularly fond of portrait painting, I liked the invitation. I knew the country round Wildwood Chase was beautiful, famous for its roses and nightingales. In a few weeks the latter would have left off singing; I should be in time to hear their richest notes. There was also a good gallery of pictures at Wildwood. In a short time my arrangements were made, and I was in the train, spinning through fields and woods in their freshest verdure, and among hedges white and fragrant with the hawthorn in full bloom.

I found the great house full of people. Lord Wylder was a genial old man, who had a large family of children and grandchildren whom he loved to gather round him, and the portrait I was to paint was intended for one of his daughters, who had lately been married. His kind flattery of my works gave me a sort of distinction in the eyes of the company, and nothing could be pleasanter than the position in which I found myself. I had a charming studio overhanging a green retreat, through leafy rifts in which a teeming rose-garden was discernible, against a distance blotted with mingled greens and purples. Here I worked, solitary as long as I pleased, and always returning to my seclusion happier for the courtesy with which the struggling artist was treated by enthusiastic admirers of his art.

The state of my health at the moment disinclining me for the society of strangers, I lived chiefly a dream-like life of my own among the delicious summer haunts which surrounded me at Wildwood Chase.

At such a time of the year, and in such delightful relations with nature, if one has not actually a close sympathetic companionship with some other living creature, one is apt to create something of the kind out of one's own imagination, and with this reflection I accounted to myself for my extraordinary attraction towards a certain picture in the gallery, the head and shoulders of a girl set against a background of the woven boughs of trees. The face had a mysterious charm impossible to describe, and was slightly leaned forward, looking straight at the gazer with an expression which seemed to me as though the creature were longing to whisper a secret. The wide over-shadowed grey eyes had a spiritual intensity such as I had never seen in any woman's face, while the sweet parted lips promised that, strong as imagination and mind might be in the character, the heart would always have the casting-vote if ever intellect and feeling should come in conflict. The hair was light, like new-mown hay, and lay in soft drifts across the delicate forehead. The peculiarity of the picture was that, wherever you moved in the gallery within sight of it, the eyes followed you with wonderful changes of expression. Sometimes they were sad and wistful, sometimes smiling, as if in mischievous amusement, and again they had a high strange outlook that tantalised you with a desire to follow it.

I ascertained that this was the portrait of a young girl of Lord Wylder's family, who had lived and died about a hundred years ago. Somehow I felt pleased that she had died early. There were portraits of beautiful women all round, who had been the grandmothers and great-grandmothers of the Wylders, caught here in their lovely girlhood, and perpetuated in youth for the eyes of posterity; but they did not interest me, and I smiled at my own satisfaction in the knowledge that my leaf-embowered goddess had never been promoted while on earth to wifehood, motherhood, and great-grandmotherhood. She had come up like a flower, appeared like the leaves on the boughs from among which her face looked forth, and even as flower and leaf she had vanished, after a short sweet summer of life, with the dews still fresh on the roses of her tender lips and cheeks.

She was a fitting companion and friend, I thought, for one like me, living a saddened ideal life, threatened with disease, overshadowed by death, uncertain of more than a very short duration of mortal existence. Smiling at this conceit, I visited her every evening at twilight, vowing vows to her, and making believe to be her lover. She had been dust already for nearly a century, and I should be dust perhaps before another year. Therefore I said we should be lovers.

Though always in love with love, I had never loved any woman in my life before, so that the June romance, sprung among roses and nightingales, and woven round the dream-maiden in the gallery nook whose eyes were dust, and whose voice (what a low sweet voice it must have been!) would never more be heard on earth, was perfectly satisfactory, inexpressibly consoling and delightful to me.

A man can hardly confess all the weak things he does when, being in low health, and tired of pretending to be strong, the child in his nature, never quite lost in any of us, rises irresistibly and asserts itself. In such a mood he will cry like a girl over a lock of his dead mother's hair, or babble to himself words of tenderness heard long ago, and only grown precious to memory in the hour of desolation. In such mood I raved softly in the dusk and solitude to my little love, with the hair like new-mown hay and the eyes that seemed to listen to me and answer me.

One evening, when I was in a particularly fantastic humour, I began to wonder if the spirit that had lived in the creature knew anything of this wayward devotion of mine, and whether, in case she did, she would be pleased or displeased at it. Upon this, the idea that my dream-love was after all no dream, but a living being in another world, which might be only separated from us by the veils upon our eyes, struck me with a force which was a very new and strange experience. It was as if she had indeed been spiritually present, and had made her presence felt by me. I thought, how strange that, were she to make herself visibly known to me, it might be only anticipating matters, seeing that in a short time I should be thoroughly qualified to join her where she abode, and I formed a distinct wish that Mayflower (so she was named), with the eyes of spiritual meaning and the brow like that of a child-angel, would come and confer with me here in the shadows, and tell me that secret, perhaps the secret of immortality, which it had seemed to me when I first saw her that she was longing to unfold.

I had turned away and walked the length of the gallery, charmed with and half smiling at my fancy, and I was within a few yards of the door, when it opened noiselessly and quickly; there was a grey flutter of drapery, shone through by the early-risen moon, which looked towards me from beyond the window in the passage on which the end of the gallery gave. I saw a young light-tinted head set against the glistening moon, which formed a golden disc behind it. I saw the spiritual gleam of eyes clear like water; I saw shoulders of a peculiar outline, and a light gossamer swathing them; and then the door shut, leaving me nothing but the living glance that had been flung towards me from the very face which I had adored and apostrophised on the canvas, now hidden by twilight at the more distant extremity of the gallery.

I remained standing where I was for several minutes. Fantastic as my humour had been, it had not been insane, but now I asked myself whether I had suddenly passed the boundary of sanity. That I had seen a vision of the girl Mayflower, who had bloomed a hundred years ago, there could be no doubt, but whether the vision was conjured up by my own disordered mind was a question which troubled me impertinently. I had not been led to expect that my mind was bound to decay sooner than my body, yet I had seen the spirit of Mayflower whom I had adjured to come to me. I believed that I had positively adjured her. And she had come.

Insomnia was part of the ailment from which I suffered, but at Wildwood I had found it scarcely irksome to lie awake and hear all the rich full sounds of the life of the summer night—the occasional rapture of the nightingale, the urgent cry of the landrail in the grass, the distant lowing of cattle, the rustling of the woods. On this night the marvel of Mayflower's spiritual apparition absorbed me; she seemed to float through the air of the midsummer night and dawn, drawing me towards her. During the next week I was feverish, impatient, altogether the worse instead of the better for my absence from London. In my calmer moments I thought of breaking my engagements, pretending inability to work on the portrait, packing up, and returning to London. The reason was that I made up my mind that the vision I had seen was a real vision, and that I was hungering to see it again. Therefore I would escape while I still had a remnant of sanity.

I did not go, however, for the insanity kept me rooted to the spot. A week passed, and the weird impression I had received was becoming a little weakened. Occasionally I admitted to myself that my imagination had played me a trick. One night, in a more than ordinarily rational frame of mind, and tired of lying awake, I rose, and letting myself out by a garden door, went for a long ramble through the park and out on the open downs, where the first faint breaking of dawn overtook me.

It was just during that spell of visible darkness which is the forerunner of the return of light, and while I stood on the verge of a small ragged-edged lake, skirted by trees and bushes—stood smoking calmly, and expectant of nothing but the sunrise, that I had my second vision of the spirit of Mayflower. I dropped my cigar, and stood breathless, as the first flutter of the slim robe came out of the tall rushes, and I beheld her floating towards me, clad in long light garments, her small head set backwards, her sweet eyes wide open, and full of that expression which in the picture most fascinated me—the high, strange, far-looking gaze which had so followed me at times that I felt utterly unable to escape from it. Her hands gathered the folds of her dress on her breast, as in the picture, and she went by with a gliding movement, like a mist-wreath. I looked her in the face, advanced towards her, involuntarily, stepped aside as she took no notice of me, and finally let her pass, daunted by her unconsciousness or indifference. No sooner had she passed than I sprang to follow her. I would speak to her at any cost. I made a spring to reach a mound in front of her, where I might again wait and watch her approach, but missed my footing and fell. When I had got upon my feet again she was gone.

The next day I laid down my brushes, and told my sitter and host that I felt I was going to be ill, and had better be at home. I went back to London, and had my illness—typhoid fever, the doctor said; and I was extremely shaken when convalescent. To my great surprise the doctor informed me that this illness had been of much service to me, and that, though weak and needing care, I was no longer in danger of consumption. If cautious I might live to be a vigorous man.

Extremely cheered by the news, I began to look back upon my experiences of Wildwood Chase as part of the hallucinations of the fever that had long been creeping over me, and with a smile and a sigh for Mayflower and her mysterious dream-sympathy, I dismissed the little romance from my reinvigorated mind. By Christmas-time I was completely recovered, and was gratified by receiving a note from Lord Wylder regretting my illness, and hoping that I would run down to Wildwood during the holidays for a change of air. He wrote from Florence, saying the Chase was deserted this winter, but the housekeeper had received orders to make me comfortable. My first impulse was to decline the invitation, but on second thoughts I decided to seize the opportunity of laying in a store of strength for coming work, and of looking on the picture of Mayflower once more, this time with the eyes of bodily and mental sanity.

After the day of my arrival had been arranged, something occurred to detain me in London, and I wrote to the housekeeper naming a later date. Within two days of the later period I found myself free, and telegraphed that I was coming twenty-four hours sooner than had been my latest intention. Owing to the snow, which had fallen in the country before it appeared in London, it happened that my telegram was not received, but of that I knew nothing as I made my way along roads just cleared for travellers, and arrived at my destination, unexpected.

The avenue had not been cleared, and leaving the trap which had brought me from the station at the lower gates, I walked by the shortest way to the house, went in by the open back way, ascended to the great hall without meeting any one, deposited my wrappings and rugs, and proceeded to make myself at home, awaiting the appearance of the housekeeper. Seeing firelight under the not quite closed door of the library, I turned in there, and glancing round the brown-panelled room, book-lined and irradiated with firelight, I saw a figure rise from the hearthrug, and stand in a wavering attitude, like a wild bird poising for flight. The form of the head and shoulders was weirdly familiar, the shine of the eyes fell on me, like a blinding revelation of things inconceivable. This was Mayflower, seen actually as if in the flesh, not by the ghost-seeing eyes of disease, but by the eyes of healthy manhood. So real was she, that after a long pause of surprise, incredulity, ending in complete assurance, I uttered some words of apology for disturbing a lady, and then remained gazing at her to see what she would do.

A few murmured words in Mayflower's true voice—the voice I had endowed her with, but had never heard before—came towards me. What they were I did not catch, but the sound acted on me like a spell, and I stood silently gazing at her as she went past me, and disappeared out of the library.

When she was gone I wakened up and rang the bell, and in a few minutes the housekeeper appeared, bearing lights, and full of apologies. She had not expected me that day; she must have misunderstood.

I made my explanations, and then asked her as unconcernedly as I could who the lady was whom I feared my unlooked-for arrival had disturbed.

"Oh, that is Miss Mayflower," she said. "She loves this library, and lives in it mostly when she gets the house to herself. If you had come tomorrow, sir, as we expected, you would not have caught sight of Miss Mayflower."

"Do you mean the lady whose portrait is in the gallery?"

"Well, it is her portrait; everybody says so. It proves her to be a true Wylder, orphan though she may be. These likenesses do turn up after a hundred years or more. There's Lady Gwendolen is the very image of her grandmother in the powdered hair in the left-hand corner as you go out at the drawing-room end."

"I thought I had seen all Lord Wylder's grand-daughters," I said, with an unaccountable sinking of the heart.

"Oh, she's none of them, poor child; only the daughter of a far-off branch of the family, and was left in care of Lord Wylder as a charity, and has been educated to be a governess. When her health is a little stronger the ladies will get her a good appointment; meantime she's here in my charge, and enjoys herself well when the family are all away from home. She's too shy to appear when there's company about the place."

I reflected, and drew rapid conclusions.

"She was here during my visit last summer!" I said.

"She was here and not very well, and I was greatly concerned about her. Her delicacy took an awkward turn; she walked in her sleep, and if I hadn't watched her something would have happened to her. Once I found she had been out of the house at night, and might have walked into the lake, or killed herself by falling down a bank. It was a serious anxiety to me, and I did not like to tell the family. She's cured of it now, I am glad to say, and will very soon be able to go out into the world for herself. Not that I shall be pleased to lose her, for I am really fond of Miss Mayflower."

The rest is too sacred to be told; but Mayflower is now the name of my wife. As I look at her this moment she is less mysterious, less dream-like than my first love in the gallery; her cheeks have a warmer tint, her eyes a happier light than the eyes like grey water, which still look stirlessly out from the newly leaved boughs of a hundred springs ago, among the shadows of the old walls of Wildwood Chase. But the likeness of feature is wonderful; and there, now, as the little head, thatched with new-mown hay, is lifted under my scrutiny, the very eager whispering look of the picture comes out on the face, and while the smile on her lips fades in wistful wonder, I remember, with a sort of awe mixed with delight, how I twice looked on this living and blooming creature of the flesh, and was fantastic enough to mistake her for a disembodied spirit.

The Lady Tantivy

Had I been napping? My head had fallen back, and my cap was awry. I had been in the garden all the afternoon gathering roses for *pot-pourri*, hoping that the absent might one day return to enjoy it, and thankful for occupation, as the summer days were long and lonesome in this remote spot, this great unpeopled house. When one is tired one easily falls asleep. But, then, how could I have been awakened by the horn of a coach?

Yet there it came again. Even in these days of extraordinary enterprise, who would run a coach through our out-of-the-world bit of country—a solitude leading, as one might say, from nowhere to nowhere else?

I put my cap straight and stood at the window, while again, louder and clearer, sounded the unusual music on the summer evening air. I left my sitting-room and stood at the open door of the great hall and looked out. Between mountainous walls of dark trees poured an avenue of sunshine across that bend in the hills where the sun was setting. Not from that side was the sound coming; but there again—tantivy—tantivy—tantivy! from the winding road that skirts the long miles of downs lying between us and ——shire. My ears strained to catch the cheerful echo, and I wished I were a passenger by that coach out into the lively world. But another blast of the bugle and the roll of quick coming wheels, startlingly near, assured me that the coach in question had turned in at our gates, and was posting towards me.

I stepped forward and strained my neck to see the first appearance of the vehicle as it rounded the corner of the broad drive; and here it came, speeding towards the house, as fine a specimen of a four-in-hand as ever was turned out in style by a coaching club. It was covered with passengers on the outside, and faces were looking laughingly out of the windows. They had all the air of gay ladies and gentlemen out for amusement. As they drove up with a long flourishing blast of the horn, I was struck by the eccentricity of the dress of this coaching company: the men in peculiarly shaped hats, high-collared coats and tight waists, the ladies with immense bonnets and scanty skirts. The horses were foaming, and I thought of the stables without grooms, nobody about but an old gardener and myself, and one woman-servant. I advanced a step, but nobody seemed to be looking at me, or even to perceive me. When the coach stopped a gentleman descended from the box-seat, opened the door of the coach, and handed out a lady, closed the door again, conducted her to the hall-door steps, left her there, and immediately remounted to his own seat. The driver gathered up the reins, the horn was blown, and the horses started. In a few moments the coach was out of sight, the sound of the retreating bugle grew fainter and fainter, and the lady remained standing on the doorsteps, alone and with her back to me.

When the horn was no longer audible she turned round, and came tripping up the steps, a charming young figure, her white muslin gown crisp and fresh with little frills and furbelows such as I had seen in pictures of my grandmother's days. Her blue sash and the little silk bag of the colour of forget-me-nots that hung from her waist had a coquettish grace, matching the curve of her long slender neck, round which golden ringlets clung, and the arch smile on her rose-mouth and in the eyes that were looking up at me. Her head-dress, a peculiar basket-like object, hung from her arm, as did a long, slim, white scarf of some silken fabric.

"I am coming to spend a night with you," she said, so sweetly that I was captivated at once. "I have travelled from what would seem to you a distance—"

"Pray come in, though I cannot promise you much in the way of entertainment," I said. "I am only caretaker in the home of my relative, who is abroad—unfortunately." My sigh, and the word "unfortunately" would, I hoped, remind her of the misfortunes of our house, of which she had probably heard.

"I know all about it," she answered. "I am a member of the family. As I said, I have come a long way, according to your ideas, to spend a night with you. Will you take me all over the old house, and talk to me about the family? I am more interested than I can tell you in the fortunes of my kindred."

"But, my dear child," I said, "where have you come from, if I may ask, and—pardon me—but how am I to know—?"

"That I am not a robber? Sit up, and watch all night— you and your servant and the old gardener. I am only one girl against the three of you. But, cousin, give me better treatment than this. You need have no doubt of me."

I felt ashamed of what she had seen in my eyes, and, wondering still at her reticence, I ran over in my mind an outline of the various far-out branches of the family tree, trying to guess which of them had dropped me this blossom. I could not recall that any of my distant cousins owned a daughter of her age.

"No," she said, seeming, as before, to answer my thought, "you cannot place me among our relatives, and I do not intend to enlighten you tonight. Tomorrow you shall know more about me. In the meantime, take me round the old garden before the daylight goes, and tell me everything you can about the present-day family."

I thought "present-day" a curious term to use, but noticing that she replied to my questions without informing me as to the point, I put on my cloak and gathered up my skirts, and led the way through the dewy alleys of green to the great old garden, which had of late become almost a wilderness. As we went she put her arm through mine, and with a curious thrill I noticed that I did not feel her do so, but only saw the action.

"You know, I dare say, that the present owner of this house is in trouble and in exile?" I explained.

"About a will," she remarked.

"An ancient will and title-deed. The documents were lost a hundred years ago."

"A hundred and nine years to the day," she replied, smiling at me.

"You are singularly accurate," I said; "but the chief thing that matters is the loss."

"How have they got on without it for a hundred years?"

"There was no one to dispute their right; but within the last few years a distant relative has sprung up and laid claim to what he declares was the inheritance of his grandfather. He pretends that the lost will was made in favour of this ancestor. He has succeeded in so far that he has got the estate into Chancery, and my cousin, having first been impoverished by years of law expenditure, has had to quit his old home with his wife and children, and is living almost in poverty in an obscure part of France."

I spoke with tears, and the bright eyes of my companion flashed sunshine into my face.

"You are tenderly attached to your cousin?"

"You may say so. My own story is an unhappy one, and when I became a widow I should have been homeless had not Geoffry Wetherwilder taken me in. I have lived in the family for years, and even now, when they have had to give up everything, he has contrived to secure me a shelter as caretaker of the Hall."

"Worthy Wetherwilders, both of you," said the girl, who also claimed to be a Wetherwilder, and she stooped to gather a splendid rose of the old, almost obsolete oriflamme, which was just in flower all over the Maiden's Bower, close to the French rosary. "How well I remember this rose!" and she kissed it.

"You have been here before!" I exclaimed in astonishment.

"Have I not! The happiest hours of my short life were spent in this garden."

"Really!"

" 'Twas this rose that Geoffry Wetherwilder gave me, the evening—just such a June evening as this—when he told me he loved me; just a hundred and eight years ago."

I stared at her, and laughed. "What are you saying?" I asked impatiently.

"Perhaps I am talking poetry," she said; "may not one do so in such a spot, on such an evening, and after—?"

Her eyes roved over the garden, taking in all its beauties, and with a look behind their youthful brightness, of age and memory, which amazed and perplexed me.

"Talk as you please," I said, but I began to feel her uncanny.

"I have only a short time to be with you," she said quickly. "Let us enjoy it. I have been very happy in this place, though not so happy as we are now—I and my beloved. But love never forgets, and the things and places associated with it are eternally sweet. I shall take him these roses, and even in the place where we are now—"

I was trying to believe that here, in the days before I came to Wetherwilder Hall, this creature's romance had been enacted, though her apparent youth made folly of the idea. But

I was growing quite bewildered by her looks and words, and was glad when she consented to leave the fading glories and the fragrance of the garden and to return with me indoors.

My handmaiden had provided a hasty supper—one or two light dishes, a sweetmeat, and grapes, coffee and shortbread. A great silver candelabra, with wax candles alight, stood in the middle of the round table in my sitting-room, which overlooked the garden, beyond which the great mounds of the trees were black against a golden stretch of sky. The flames of the candles hung like flowers in the air, for the gold sky-gleam was still at least equal with them in power of light within the room, and both together filled the place with a kind of mystic glamour.

We sat down to table, but I was too much excited to eat, and my guest, though plates were placed before her, seemed to behave as if they contained nothing but air. However, I had become afraid of observing her too closely, so quickly did she apprehend my thought, and I allowed myself to drift with her humour.

After supper she protested that she must see the old house, and so we proceeded upstairs just as the newly burnished moon-silver began to struggle in the sky with the sun-gold which was rusting away into darkness down west among wildernesses of grotesque-seeming ink-black oak woods. The white glory poured down the wide way of the great staircase as we went up; corridors, passages, and unused chambers lay beyond and above. I felt that I would rather have remained downstairs, but my companion hurried on, looking round here, and peeping in there, as if truly revisiting places that were dear and familiar to her.

She lingered only about a minute in each spot until we came to a small music-room, all brown with polished wood, without curtains or carpet, and hung round with musical instruments, some of them very old, an accumulation of years. Violin, guitar, mandolina, tambourine, cymbals, all were there, and an old-fashioned spinet and a harp held place of honour in the middle of the floor.

With an air of rapture she stepped a-tiptoe across the floor, stretched her long delicate arm to take down the guitar from its hanging place, and slipping a faded blue ribbon that dangled from it over her head, she perched herself on a carved wooden stool, and sung with the most exquisite grace a soft, cooing love-song, the like of which for sweetness I had never listened to. When the piercing melody ceased she looked up at me, and never shall I forget the beauty of her as she did so, with the moonlight that struck through the narrow window just touching her face and shoulder. Her song sung, she replaced the guitar on the wall, and turning to me with a little laugh signed to me that she desired to quit the chamber.

Proceeding with our visitation we made little pause till we reached another small room, one which had been for generations a kind of schoolroom or study for the young people of the family. It was lined with books, and a table with drawers stood in the middle of the floor. Here had many a lesson been learned, and many a lecture listened to. Again, as in the music-room, the stranger's look of recognition became rapturous, as she walked round the rows of books with her eyes close to them, though I could scarcely imagine that the twilight from the window enabled her to read the titles of them.

Suddenly she drew forth from a corner, where it had evidently lain hid behind others, a small vellum-covered volume, and with a laugh of delight turned its pages over with a rapid hand, then placed it in mine with an eager movement, saying:

"Take it, cousin, and tomorrow look into it. It will explain away your perplexity."

I was growing weary of following her, of my ignorance of who she was and why she was here; and my wits were oppressed by the consciousness of something about her which I found quite unintelligible. I longed to be alone, that away from the fascination of her presence I might think the matter over, and arrive at some conclusion regarding her. I was, therefore, much relieved when she suddenly announced that she would retire for the night.

"Give me the yellow chamber," she said with her charming imperiousness.

I knew that my maid had prepared for her a smaller room and nearer to my own, and remarked that she might perhaps feel lonesome in the greater apartment, which was situated at the other end of the house. But she reiterated her request, which was rather, indeed, a demand. In a short time the statelier chamber was made ready for her, and I accompanied her there. The yellow hangings on the bed and windows were let down and shaken out, but she would not allow the blinds to be drawn or the windows closed.

It is a splendid old room, the walls completely panelled in oak, the darkness of which is relieved by the gold-colour of the furniture. She bade me goodnight, bending to kiss me, but I did not feel her lips, and experienced again that uncanny thrill at finding my sense of touch unaffected by her nearness. I last saw her standing there with her graceful arms extended dismissing me. Two candles were burning in the tall silver candlesticks on the dressing-table; the moon, full-orbed and glorious, shone out of the lovely green-greyness of the sky of a midsummer midnight, filling the framework of one window, while the other window showed the startling black fretwork formed by the huge boughs of a hundred-year-old chestnut tree against the silvery cloud-light. Between these and the flames of the candles the young slight figure stood, aerial in its lightness and grace, the face radiant with intelligence, the eyes of a brightness which seemed strange by such light as there was, the moon's soft ray making a luminous ring round her hair. She kissed her hand to me with a smile that is still in my heart; and then I closed the door and retreated to my own quarters, glad to escape, and feeling indescribably limp and overdone.

I did not find my brain cleared by solitude as immediately and effectively as I had hoped, and felt unable to do anything but huddle myself up in bed with a sense of the most utter prostration. After half an hour's rest I sat up and lit my candle, polished my spectacles, and opened the vellum-covered book which the stranger had handed to me. But whether from fatigue or for some other reason, I could not read a word of the contents, and soon consigned myself once more to repose and darkness.

Sleep took me by surprise, and I knew no more till I wakened with a thin clear sound in my ears, curiously familiar as the repetition of something I had been aware of very lately. It was the lively sound of a coach-horn blown from a distance. Again it came lightly, and again and again more faintly on the air—tantivy, tantivy, tantivy! The great cedar outside flung its boughs about in the breeze, and their rustling drowned the retreating music. I sat up, and saw that the light of a midsummer dawn was gilding the edges of the window-blinds.

I dressed hurriedly, and feeling a strange reluctance to visiting the yellow chamber, I wakened my maidservant and directed her to make me a strong cup of tea, which I swallowed nervously. The maid was a sturdy country wench, devoid of imagination, and she smiled at my discomfiture.

"It's my belief you won't find her, ma'am," she said. "They gay friends of hers called for her and took her off, early. I heard the coachin'-horn an hour ago, comin' an' comin', and goin' an' goin'. I put my head out of the winda, and I saw the coach, and the waft of her white gown gettin' into it; and the whole caravan went clatterin' down the drive and out of sight among the trees just as the sun was risin'. And I wouldn't be frettin' for her, if I was you, ma'am, for she's a queer kind of a visitor, takin' people short and givin' them trouble, and then goin' off without as much as saying good morning to them!"

"Come upstairs with me, Jenny, that I may assure myself she is gone," I said.

We entered the room. The windows still stood wide open, but their dark woodwork framed the brilliant sunshine and blue sky of a June morning. Rooks were cawing in the huge chestnut, which threw half the room into transparent shadow. The room was empty of its occupant of the night before. The bed had not been lain in, and everything stood undisturbed, as I had left it with her in it. And yet there was a change, for one of the panels in the wooded wall stood open as a door, showing a deep recess like a cupboard, about five feet above the level of the floor.

Thrilling with expectation of I knew not what, I looked into the open recess, and putting in my hand drew forth an Indian box containing some old yellow papers, the miniature of a girl, which was a faithful portrait of my late guest, and a few jewels in old-fashioned settings. Having read the papers, I telegraphed at once to Geoffry Wetherwilder, and to his solicitor, and both arrived as quickly as steam could carry them. The papers found proved to be the long-lost will, so urgently needed for the welfare of our family.

It was long before I ventured to relate to my cousin, or to his man of business, the story of the finding of the document as I have set it down here. When I did so each received my communication characteristically. The solicitor laughed and tapped his forehead with an amused glance at me. "Don't tell that monstrous tale again, my dear lady," he said, "for I can't undertake to defend you from the consequences."

He accepted as quite natural the finding of the papers behind a sliding panel, but the rest he put down to a dream.

Geoffry, on the contrary, heard my story with the most serious attention, and received it as truth in all its details. He had the Celtic strain in him which readily responds to a message from the unknown. The spiritual side of his nature was deeply stirred, and having been made suddenly very happy just when his fortunes looked darkest, the heart in him turned gratefully, like my own, to the lovely visitant from another state of being, who had taken thought of him and his, and restored them to their own.

"Don't say a word of it to Vanda, however," he said, speaking of his wife, who was already on her joyful way home, with her little children. "The thought of such an occurrence in the house would be an everlasting terror to her." And the mistress of Wetherwilder remains in ignorance of the story to this day.

The vellum-covered book proved to be a diary kept in disjointed, schoolgirl fashion. Inside the cover was written, "Elsinore Wetherwilder, aged seventeen today. Called by some impertinent cousins 'the Lady Tantivy', because she loves riding to hunt, and in a four-in-hand coach." And after this was added in a masculine youthful hand: "and sometimes even insists upon blowing the horn!"

The first entry was of an earlier date than the inscription on the cover:

"This week I have arrived at Wetherwilder Hall. It is a change indeed for an orphan girl leaving her convent school with no family or relatives to receive her. What should I have done, where should I have gone, had not the dear old Squire arrived at Avignon, and put me in his portmanteau and carried me home? Really, and really home. And such a home!

"I am wild with delight. I have a ready-made mother, and the big-boy cousins are brothers to me. And the best of it is they are all as happy as I am, for the Wetherwilders had no daughter until I came."

Various girlish and pretty writings followed, filling up a year. In the first winter, this:

"The snow is deep, yet the ball came off. The squire gave me a wonder of a white satin dress. My head is turned with flatteries. The duke proposed to me, but I should have refused him had he been king of the world, and that though he is a very goodly gentleman. It is Geoffry that I love, and never another man than Geoffry. If Geoffry does not love me, then will I go back to my convent at Avignon and cover up this golden hair with a nun's veil—"

The next summer:

"This evening Geoffry told me that he loved me. It was in the garden among the oriflamme roses. I knew it before, but it was sweet to hear it—"

In the following autumn:

"I have been trying to plague Geoffry. He is so sweet-tempered one can hardly do it. I have hidden the will and documents he was showing me yesterday. I have put them behind the sliding panel in the yellow chamber, where I am now installed. As all his inheritance depends on them, he will be rather in a fright. I will tease him for a while, and then make amends by being ever so kind to him."

No more. Each time I close the little book, which I always keep by me with the miniature, I think I hear the faint horn blowing that announced the coming and going of my Lady Tantivy. She will never come again. When we meet, it must be that I shall go to her. Time and place are delusions. I am very old now, and as I gaze over the trees into the great space out of which she came in her ever-young delightfulness, my heart grows young and is glad.

Acknowledgments

This volume was originally published by Sarob Press as the eighth instalment in their "Mistresses of the Macabre" series, edited by Richard Dalby.

I am thankful to those who assisted with this previous edition: Barry Cross, Michael Flowers, Paul Lowe, and Sara Morgan. I am particularly indebted to Robert Morgan, who generously provided me with the story texts; and, of course, to the friendship and undying scholarship of the late Richard Dalby.

I would also like to extend my gratitude, for this new edition, to the Estate of Richard Dalby: Jean and Joe Conway, and Mark Conway; to Brian Coldrick for his fine cover art, and to the Swan River team: Meggan Kehrli, Ken Mackenzie, and Jim Rockhill.

Not to Be Taken at Bed-Time & Other Strange Stories
was originally published by
Sarob Press, Neuilly-le-Vendin (2013).

❧

"Not to Be Taken at Bed-Time"
All the Year Round,
Christmas Number (1865).

Acknowledgments

"The Ghost at the Rath"
All the Year Around (14 April 1866).

"The Haunted Organist of Hurly Burly"
All the Year Round (19 November 1866).

"The Mystery of Ora"
All the Year Round,
Extra Summer Number (1 July 1879).

"A Strange Love Story"
All the Year Round,
Extra Summer Number (3 July 1882).

"The Ghost at Wildwood Chase"
Illustrated Almanac & Annual (1888).

"The Lady Tantivy"
Temple Bar (January 1898).

About the Author

Rosa Mulholland was born in Belfast on 19 March 1841. In 1891 she married the eminent Irish historian Sir John T. Gilbert (1829-1898). In addition to her two-volume *Life of Sir John T. Gilbert* (1905), Mulholland produced a long line of novels mostly set in rural Ireland, and featuring strong female characters, including *The Wicked Woods of Tobereevil* (1872) and *Banshee Castle* (1895). Many of her supernatural tales were collected in *The Haunted Organist of Hurly Burly* (1880). Mulholland died at her home Villa Nova on 21 April 1921.

About the Editor

Richard Dalby (1949-2017), born in London, was a widely-respected editor, anthologist, and scholar of supernatural fiction. He has edited collections by E. F. Benson, Bram Stoker, and Rosa Mulholland; and his numerous anthologies include *Dracula's Brood*, *Victorian Ghost Stories by Eminent Women Writers*, and *Victorian and Edwardian Ghost Stories*.

SWAN RIVER PRESS

Founded in 2003, Swan River Press is an independent publishing company, based in Dublin, Ireland, dedicated to gothic, supernatural, and fantastic literature. We specialise in limited edition hardbacks, publishing fiction from around the world with an emphasis on Ireland's contributions to the genre.

www.swanriverpress.ie

"Handsome, beautifully made volumes . . . altogether irresistible."

– Michael Dirda, *Washington Post*

"It [is] often down to small, independent, specialist presses to keep the candle of horror fiction flickering . . . "

– Darryl Jones, *Irish Times*

"Swan River Press has emerged as one of the most inspiring new presses over the past decade. Not only are the books beautifully presented and professionally produced, but they aspire consistently to high literary quality and originality, ranging from current writers of supernatural/weird fiction to rare or forgotten works by departed authors."

– Peter Bell, *Ghosts & Scholars*

BENDING TO EARTH
Strange Stories by Irish Women

edited by Maria Giakaniki
and Brian J. Showers

Irish women have long produced literature of the gothic, uncanny, and supernatural. *Bending to Earth* draws together twelve such tales. While none of the authors herein were considered primarily writers of fantastical fiction during their lifetimes, they each wandered at some point in their careers into more speculative realms—some only briefly, others for lengthier stays.

Names such as Charlotte Riddell and Rosa Mulholland will already be familiar to aficionados of the eerie, while Katharine Tynan and Clotilde Graves are sure to gain new admirers. From a ghost story in the Swiss Alps to a premonition of death in the West of Ireland to strange rites in a South Pacific jungle, *Bending to Earth* showcases a diverse range of imaginative writing which spans the better part of a century.

> "Bending to Earth *is full of tales of women walled-up in rooms, of vengeful or unforgetting dead wives, of mistreated lovers, of cruel and murderous husbands.*"
>
> – Darryl Jones, *Irish Times*

> "*A surprising, extraordinary anthology featuring twelve uncanny and supernatural stories from the nineteenth century . . . highly recommended, extremely enjoyable.*"
>
> – *British Fantasy Society*

"NUMBER NINETY"
& Other Ghost Stories

B. M. Croker

The bestselling Irish author B. M. Croker enjoyed a highly successful literary career from 1880 until her death forty years later. Her novels were witty and fast moving, set mostly in India and her native Ireland. Titles such as *Proper Pride* (1882) and *Diana Barrington* (1888) found popularity for their mix of romantic drama and Anglo-Indian military life. And, like many late-Victorian authors, Croker also wrote ghost stories for magazines and Christmas annuals. From the colonial nightmares such as "The Dâk Bungalow at Dakor" and "The North Verandah" to the more familiar streets of haunted London in "Number Ninety", this collection showcases fifteen of B. M. Croker's most effective supernatural tales.

"This is a solid collection of stories that deserve to be better known . . . they are all enjoyable ghostly tales, and ideal reading for the long winter nights."

– Supernatural Tales

"[Croker's] Indian stories evoke colonial life vividly . . . What makes them all readable are the well-observed characters and settings"

– Wormwood

THE DEATH SPANCEL
and Others

Katharine Tynan

Katharine Tynan is not a name immediately associated with the supernatural. However, like many other writers of the early twentieth century, she made numerous forays into literature of the ghostly and macabre, and throughout her career produced verse and prose that conveys a remarkable variety of eerie themes, moods, and narrative forms. From her early, elegiac stories, inspired by legends from the West of Ireland, to pulpier efforts featuring grave-robbers and ravenous rats, Tynan displays an eye for weird detail, compelling atmosphere, and a talent for rendering a broad palette of uncanny effects. *The Death Spancel and Others* is the first collection to showcase Tynan's tales of supernatural events, prophecies, curses, apparitions, and a pervasive sense of the ghastly.

"Of remarkably high literary quality . . . a great collection recommended to any good fiction lover."

– Mario Guslandi

"Tynan's fiction is of a high standard, crafted in relatively simple yet still lyrical prose . . . a very assured craftswoman of the supernatural tale."

– Supernatural Tales

"Lovers of late Victorian and Edwardian ghost fiction will assuredly adore the restrained literary quality . . ."

– The Pan Review